As the buggy raced west along the dirt carriage road, Edward Trenary thought of his meeting with Alvin McNally. He neither liked nor trusted the man, yet he had no choice but to use him. Only McNally commanded a gang sufficiently large to pull off a caper of this sort.

"One more time," he told himself with a smile. "After tonight, one more should be enough."

Ahead he could see the small twin bridges that traversed Box Elder Creek, the left one for road traffic, the right for trains. He did not see the Denver-bound freight train anywhere near the bridge, which could mean only one thing. . . .

Trenary's thought was confirmed by a sudden, thunderous explosion a mile or so down the track. There were a number of smaller explosions, and then a brilliant flash of light that lit the morning sky. He wanted to see the wreck up close while the flames were at their peak. And then he had to put a good fifteen miles behind him so that he could be in Denver when word arrived of this latest mysterious tragedy.

FARADAY #2

COLLISION COURSE

William Grant

™ **BCI** Created by the producers of **Wagons West, Stagecoach, Badge,** and **White Indian.**

Book Creations Inc., Canaan, NY · Lyle Kenyon Engel, Founder

LYNX BOOKS
New York

FARADAY #2: COLLISION COURSE

ISBN: 1-55802-182-5

First Printing/September 1988

Produced by Book Creations, Inc.
Founder: Lyle Kenyon Engel

This book is published by Lynx Books, a division of Lynx Communications, Inc., 41 Madison Avenue, New York, New York, 10010. The name "Lynx" together with the logotype consisting of a stylized head of a lynx is a trademark of Lynx Communications, Inc.

Printed in the United States of America

0 9 8 7 6 5 4 3 2 1

Chapter 1

THE BRIDE WAS WEARING A GOWN OF WHITE SILK, CUT TIGHT through the bodice and hips to accentuate her sleek yet curvaceous figure, then flaring at the calves and draping several inches along the floor. Her long, delicate fingers gripped a bouquet of white carnations, and her green eyes glistened with tears as she looked somewhat nervously from the priest in front of her to the man who stood beside her, ready to take his vows. Her full red lips quivered and broke into a smile. Coyly, she reached up with one hand and tucked into place a vagrant wisp of hair that had slipped from the Oriental carved-lacquer comb she had used to pull her long brunette locks into an upsweep.

The groom looked perfectly at ease in a starched, high-collar shirt and formal black suit, his string tie and black boots the only trace of his frontier upbringing. He glanced through the only clear-pane window in the church and looked down off the hill at the numerous small fishing feluccas returning to San Francisco Bay and the lone clipper ship that was following the tide out to sea. When he turned back to his bride-to-be, his pale-blue eyes seemed almost giddy with delight. In his midthirties, he was perhaps ten years older than the woman who stood with him at the altar, but his handsome, clean-shaven features and sandy-blond hair made him appear far more youthful.

The priest was a dour-looking man well past middle age. His curly gray hair was contrasted by thick black brows that protruded ominously over his heavy-lidded, equally dark eyes. He spoke in a deep, rasping voice, his words laden with portent as he recited the marriage ceremony. Only occasionally did he look up from the book in front of him to direct a severe gaze at the gathered assembly, like a father admonishing his children for acts they had not yet considered, let alone committed.

The gathering consisted of but two well-wishers, one on either side of the church. Both were young men in poorly tailored suits; they sat looking around uncomfortably, as if wondering why they alone were on hand and how best to make their escape.

Suddenly the priest slammed shut the big leather book and gripped the sides of the podium so rigidly that it shook. Leaning forward slightly, he squinted one eye and raised the opposite brow. Looking back and forth between the two men in the audience, he intoned, "If any man can show just cause why they may not lawfully be joined together, let him now speak. . . ."

The two men shifted uncomfortably in their pews, glancing first at each other and then behind them at the open doors that led from the church.

"Let him now speak!" the priest exclaimed again, pounding the podium with both fists and causing the two men to bolt upright on their benches. His final words were delivered in a dramatic whisper: "Or else hereafter forever hold his peace."

The priest's clenched hands relaxed, and what passed

for a smile briefly touched his features. He turned to the bride and said, "Do you, Nora Sutherland, take this man, Stuart Kennedy—?"

"*I* do!" a voice shouted, and everyone turned to see a burly, middle-aged man enter the rear of the church, a double-barreled shotgun cradled in his arms. "I sure as hell *do* object . . . and that bastard sure as hell knows why!" Lowering the shotgun slightly, he waved the barrels toward Stuart Kennedy.

"I see you got my invitation, Wilcox," Kennedy drawled, turning to face the man who stood now at the end of the center aisle.

"Hope you don't mind, but I brought a couple of friends." Wilcox grinned smugly and nodded over his shoulder. Two men appeared in the doorway behind him, each armed with a repeating rifle.

"Now see here," the priest began, waving a fist at the intruders. "This is a house of God. There'll be no—"

"Settle down, *padre*," Wilcox cut him off. He glanced back at his two men, who spread out on either side of him along the back of the church. "I've just come for a word with the groom and his pretty little lady," Wilcox continued, training his shotgun on the wedding party, while his men covered the two cowering guests in the pews.

"What about?" Kennedy asked.

"You damn well know. And so does *Nora*." He spat out her name as though it were poison. Turning to her, he said bitterly, "You really played me for the sucker, didn't you? A lot of sweet talk and promises, but you never did follow through. And all the while you were playing house with that—" he waggled the gun at Kennedy "—that traitorous bastard!"

"Enough of this—"

"I'll say when it's enough!" Wilcox again cut off the priest. He looked at Kennedy and gave a curt, humorless laugh. "It sure as hell took me long enough to figure out that you were the one who stole those confidential files and turned them over to the police. You played me almost as good as she did . . . but then again, you don't quite have her charms, now do you?"

"This is a church," Kennedy reminded him, keeping his tone level. "If you've got a complaint with me, it can wait till after—"

"The wedding? There's not gonna be any wedding!" Wilcox came walking up the aisle a few steps. "You've got a lot of nerve thinking I'd let you two die as husband and wife." He looked over at the priest and laughed bitterly. "She was the one who kept me busy by running her fingers through my hair while he was running his fingers through the records of my company. And after I took him in—gave him a position of responsibility on the inside." He turned to Kennedy again. "Why'd you do it? What was to gain? If you'd have stuck with me, you could've been rich. Now you're just gonna get a bellyful of buckshot. You and that two-timing woman of yours."

"No!" Nora gasped, raising a hand toward Wilcox. "It wasn't my fault. He . . . he forced me to help him."

"How?" Wilcox asked, plainly unconvinced.

Nora descended from the altar and started down the aisle until Wilcox signaled her to halt. She stood there, her hand raised in supplication. "He made me play up to you like that. I . . . I never wanted to. But he was blackmailing me."

Wilcox slowly shook his head. "You're lying. You wouldn't be here today if—"

"I had no choice. Not about what I did to you . . . not even about this wedding. He's holding all the cards."

"What cards?" Wilcox asked skeptically.

"I'll show you," Nora blurted, her eyes suddenly showing an eager light. "Then you'll see that I didn't want to hurt you."

Nora took a few more steps toward Wilcox, then raised her left foot and rested it on one of the right-hand pews. Slowly, almost seductively, she started raising the hem of her gown, unveiling a muscular, well-turned calf, which more than held the full attention of Wilcox and his two men at the rear of the church.

"I have papers right here to prove it," she said as the dress rose above her knee and slid up along her thigh, revealing a blue garter with some papers tucked underneath along the outside of her leg. "Right here," she repeated, withdrawing the papers.

"Let me see," Wilcox demanded.

Nora made no move except to hold out the papers in her left hand. Wilcox approached, his eyes alternately fixed on the papers and her shapely leg, which Nora began to caress with the fingertips of her right hand.

"This will explain everything," she whispered as he lowered the twin barrels of the shotgun and took hold of the papers. She held on to them for a moment, then finally released them.

Wilcox shook open the papers to read the contents, then quickly riffled through them. "These are blank," he declared, shaking them at her.

"But this isn't," she replied with a thin smile. It was then that Wilcox noticed that she was holding a snub-nosed revolver, which had been tucked behind the garter along her inner thigh. "Don't move," she added for emphasis, though her admonition was not really necessary, for upon seeing the gun barrel pointed at his belly, Wilcox had frozen.

Wilcox's two men did not react right away, and when one of them realized what was happening and swung his rifle toward Nora, she raised her own gun in full sight and said, "Drop it, or he dies."

The gunman hesitated, then suddenly brought up his rifle. Nora immediately swung her hand toward him and pulled the trigger, the bullet catching the gunman in the chest and throwing him back against the wall.

While Nora was preoccupied with the gunman, Wilcox took advantage of the moment and brought up his shotgun. But before he could level it at Nora, there was a burst of gunfire, with one slug tearing into his belly and another striking his shoulder and spinning him to the side. He felt the shotgun falling from his hands as he looked up in surprise and saw both the groom and the priest standing with smoking revolvers aimed at him. Cursing, he went down on one knee, then fell onto his side and just lay there, groaning with pain.

The remaining gunman was caught completely by surprise. He found himself facing five revolvers, for by now the two men in the pews had drawn weapons, as well.

"Drop it!" the woman in the wedding gown shouted as she held her revolver in both hands and aimed it at his head. "Now!"

The man did as ordered, slowly lowering the rifle and letting it slide to the floor. He made no effort to resist as the men in the pews came around and took him into custody, cuffing his hands behind his back.

Stuart Kennedy pulled open the lapel of his formal suit and slipped his Smith & Wesson revolver into a brown-leather shoulder holster. As he came down the aisle, Nora was already kneeling beside Wilcox, examining the wound in his belly. She gave Kennedy a slight shake of the head to indicate that the man would not make it.

Grimacing, Wilcox looked up at Nora, his face flush with shock and pain. He opened his mouth to speak, but she placed a hand on his shoulder and tried to ease him back against the floor in an attempt to make him as comfortable as possible.

"Wh-who?" Wilcox managed to stammer.

"I'm a Faraday agent," Nora told him. "So is Stuart."

"Faraday? Matthew F-Faraday?" he asked, naming the founder and owner of the Faraday Security Service. "B-but why?"

"We were hired by the Southern Pacific Railroad," Kennedy put in. "They suspected that your company was billing them for work never done. It wasn't until I went undercover that we realized your crimes included murder."

"The p-priest?" Wilcox gasped, looking up at the man who had been performing the wedding service and who now had removed his clerical collar and stood a short distance away.

"Sergeant Flynn of the San Francisco police force. He helped set up this little ruse of ours."

Suddenly Wilcox began to laugh, but the motion quickly set him choking and sputtering. When he had calmed down somewhat, he reached out and grabbed hold of the hem of Nora's wedding gown. "So you n-never were planning to go to bed with me, w-were you?" he said in a grating whisper, and she shook her head. "Good. You p-played so hard to get, I . . . I was afraid I'd lost my t-touch."

Wilcox's eyes fluttered and closed. Slowly his grip on Nora's wedding dress eased, and then his head lolled back and his entire body went limp.

Nora stood and slipped her arm through Kennedy's. She felt weak but knew she would not faint. No matter how much this man may have deserved his fate, it was never easy to be the cause of another's death.

"We'll have this place cleaned up in time for evening mass," Sergeant Flynn said almost casually.

"I hope the parish priest doesn't raise hell when he sees what went on here today," Kennedy put in, looking over at the bloody smear along the wall where the other gunman had fallen and died.

"Don't be worrying about Father Dunphy," Flynn assured him. "He's my wife's brother. He'll just be sorry he missed the excitement."

"Would you mind if Nora and I disappeared for a while? We'd like to wire our report to Matthew Faraday before the office in Kansas City closes."

"Just be sure to come down to the station later to sign *my* report," Flynn said. He started to lead them toward the door, then abruptly stopped and grasped Kennedy's arm.

"What is it?" Kennedy asked.

"I'd forgotten . . . we hadn't finished the ceremony."

The Faraday agents looked at each other and grinned. "I don't think that will be necessary," Nora told him.

"Are you certain?" Flynn asked with a mischievous smile. "I've heard my brother-in-law perform it enough to know it by heart. And it'd be a shame to waste those outfits of yours."

"Perhaps some other time," Kennedy replied.

Flynn gave a grunt of disapproval. "Do I at least get to kiss the bride?"

"Why, certainly, Sergeant," Nora declared, stepping close to the older man and kissing him on the cheek.

"I suppose that will have to do," he grumbled. "But if you ever decide to tie the knot, you make sure that Father Dunphy performs the ceremony and that his brother-in-law, poor old Sergeant Flynn, is given a seat in the front row."

"Flynn, old boy," Kennedy declared, slapping the policeman on the back, "if Nora and I get married, you'll be the best man."

"I already am!" Flynn exclaimed with a wry grin. "And don't you youngsters ever forget it."

He led them through the front doors and outside, where the surviving gunman was being loaded into an unmarked police wagon by the two young policemen who had served as the lone members of the wedding party.

"Where are you off to next?" Flynn asked as Nora and Kennedy started down the steps.

"It's back to Kansas City, then wherever Matthew Faraday sees fit to send us," Kennedy answered.

"Think you'll be returning to San Francisco?"

"These days most of our work is in the heart of the western frontier. The East and West coasts have gotten far too civilized."

"San Francisco?" Flynn shook his head. "Never."

"I suppose there's always room for some excitement in this town, so I'm sure we'll be back here in time."

"And when you do, make sure you look up your good friend Sergeant Flynn."

Assuring him that they would, the Faraday agents took their leave and made their way to a buggy that sat parked at the curb. After taking their seats, Kennedy picked up the reins and slapped them against the horse's back. There was a riotous clatter as the buggy pulled away and started down the road. Nora and Kennedy did not have to look behind them to realize that the policeman and his young partners had tied ribbons and tin cans to the back of the buggy, along with a hand-painted sign that proclaimed: *Just Married.*

Less than a week later, in September of 1889, Nora Sutherland was having a late dinner by herself in a crowded railroad dining car, while Stuart Kennedy remained in their private compartment working on their final report about the successful operation in San Francisco. The Union Pacific train had left Cheyenne, Wyoming, earlier in the evening and was heading south toward Denver. In the morning the agents would switch to the Kansas Pacific branch of the Union Pacific Railroad on a train bound for Kansas City, home of the Faraday Security Service.

Nora had ordered a special cut of meat and was just finishing her salad when the elderly Chinese waiter approached and said, "Excuse me, ma'am, but gentleman over there would like to share table. I tell him there will be vacant table in a few minutes, but—"

"That's quite all right," she said, glancing toward the front of the car to see a pleasant-looking young man in a brown tweed suit. He looked to be about Nora's age of twenty-six, and she guessed that they were the same height—five foot six. The stranger had brown eyes and hair and a trim mustache, and even from a distance she could see a pair of well-defined dimples as he smiled at her.

"Tell him he's welcome to join me," she informed the waiter while smiling politely at the young man.

The waiter nodded and withdrew. A moment later, the stranger came up to the table, grasped the back of the vacant chair, and asked, "May I?" When Nora nodded, he pulled it out and took his seat. "I saw you and your husband in the salon car when I boarded in Cheyenne, but we haven't been introduced. My name is Jim Hart. Thank you for your hospitality, Mrs. . . ."

"Sutherland. Nora Sutherland."

"Isn't your husband joining you for dinner?"

"He wasn't hungry—and he's not my husband. I'm traveling with my brother, Stuart Kennedy," she explained, using the cover story she and Kennedy generally adopted while on the road between assignments.

"But I thought . . ." He glanced at her left hand, which bore a wedding ring.

"I'm a widow. Stuart and I are on our way to visit relatives in Kansas City. And you?"

"I'm bound for Denver. I'm a reporter with *The Rocky Mountain News*. Some colleagues and I were in Cheyenne for the past week attending the opening of the constitutional convention."

"Does it seem likely that Wyoming will become our forty-fourth state?"

"From all the rhetoric, I'd say there's a more than even chance."

"Excellent."

"Then you approve, even though the territory has barely sixty thousand residents?" he asked.

"But of course. The territory has allowed women to vote since 1869; if admitted to the Union, it will become the first state with full women's suffrage."

"Ahh, a suffragist," he commented with what could be interpreted as a disapproving smile.

"I'm no militant," Nora avowed. "But I certainly believe in equality."

"But don't you think that in certain areas—politics, for instance—women should let men make the decisions?"

"Would you be willing to let a woman make decisions for you?" she challenged.

"Perhaps not about politics," he admitted. "But yes, in many areas I'm quite willing to accept a woman's judgment."

Just then the waiter reappeared at the table and offered a menu, but Hart waved it away, saying grandly, "I'll have whatever Mrs. Sutherland ordered." As the Chinese man padded silently away, Hart smiled at Nora. "There, do you see? I let you choose my dinner. I'm truly a suffragist at heart."

Grinning mischievously, Nora replied, "That's only because you didn't know that I've asked the waiter to prepare a special order of kou jou for me."

"Which is . . . ?" Hart raised one eyebrow uncertainly.

"In Kweilin, China, where my parents were missionaries, kou jou was the local specialty." She closed her eyes and inhaled through her nose, as if enjoying an intoxicating aroma. *"Kou jou,"* she repeated. Opening her eyes, she paused for dramatic effect and then translated, "Roast dog meat. A great delicacy, really, especially if the dog is young and plump."

As if on signal, the elderly waiter appeared with a salad in one hand and a plate of thin-cut meat in the other. "Special cut for you, ma'am," he said with a broad grin as he placed the blood-red meat in front of Nora.

"Hsieh hsieh," Nora told the waiter, thanking him in Mandarin Chinese.

The waiter's eyes widened with delight, and he replied, *"Pu k'o ch'i,"* the Mandarin equivalent for "You're welcome." He served Jim Hart his salad, then gave a low bow and departed.

"Do you mind if I start eating?" Nora asked Hart, who was staring numbly across the table at the plate of meat. "*Kou jou* gets tough and stringy if it sits uneaten for too long."

"Uh, no . . . not at all," he said, grimacing as she cut a thin slice of meat and placed it in her mouth.

"Umm . . . delicious," she fairly moaned with delight.

Trying to look away, Hart picked up his fork and toyed with his salad.

"We were discussing women's suffrage," Nora said after eating for a few minutes. "You were arguing that a woman should let a man make the important decisions for her, like I just did for you—though of course my decision was but a small, insignificant one." She took another bite of meat and waited a moment as he stared uncomfortably at her. Then she continued, "Do you still agree?"

"Why, yes, of course . . . I suppose."

"Ahh . . . here comes your *kou jou*," she announced as the waiter approached with a second portion of meat.

The young reporter felt his face flushing as the waiter set the entrée before him with a great flourish. Almost beseechingly, he looked up at the Chinese man and said in awkward Mandarin, *"Kou jou?"*

The waiter's eyebrows raised almost as far as his jaw dropped. He stared down at Hart, his face a severe mask of indignation. Reaching over, he tapped the table next to the plate and declared, "No dog meat! Delmonico steak!" Spinning around, he stormed away across the dining car, leaving Jim Hart sitting there staring after him with a sheepish expression.

It was all Nora could do to keep from bursting into a titter of laughter. "I'm sorry," she apologized, struggling to maintain her composure.

Hart sat shaking his head at her, uncertain whether to be angry or amused. Finally he gave a slight grin and muttered, "Dog meat indeed!"

"I truly am sorry," Nora apologized, "but I couldn't

help myself. I wanted you to see what it can feel like when you are forced to let someone else make the decisions—important or not."

"Your point is well taken." He picked up his fork and knife and was about to cut into the meat, but then he put them down and said, "I think I've lost my appetite."

"Don't be silly. It's perfectly fine."

"Are you sure?" he asked skeptically.

"Would I lie to you?" She giggled, then waved her fork at his plate. "Now go on. It's delicious."

Still hesitant, Hart grasped his fork and gingerly poked at the meat. Deciding that it was safe to proceed, he picked up the knife and started to make the first cut. The knife had barely sliced into the meat when Nora gave a sharp little bark and burst into laughter.

Jumping with surprise, Hart dropped the utensils and nearly knocked over his glass of water. For a long moment he sat eyeing Nora with barely contained anger, and then he began to laugh, as well.

Halfway between Cheyenne and Denver, at a point where the railroad tracks traversed the South Platte River, a slow-moving freight train was approaching the trestle bridge from the south. The bridge was being rebuilt, and during this phase of construction the north-bound track was closed, requiring traffic from both directions to use the same set of rails.

Temporary connecting tracks had been laid to shunt the northbound train onto the southbound track and then back onto its own track on the far side of the river. Special signals had been installed and connected to a pneumatic switching system. This allowed the engineer to make a single stop on the near side to manually throw the main shunting lever, which simultaneously engaged the switches on both sides of the bridge and reversed the signals. The train then could proceed forward and would automatically be shunted onto the single track and then back onto its own track after crossing the river.

Pulling on the throttle to bring the train to a halt, the engineer peered ahead through the grimy front window. He tried to wipe the glass in order to see better, then leaned out of the open side window to verify that the red signal was up, indicating that the bridge had last been used by a southbound train and that the shunting switches would have to be reversed for the northbound train to pass.

As the train slowed to a halt, the engineer turned to the fireman, the only other occupant in the locomotive, and said, "You'll have to throw the switch, Robbie."

"Sure thing, Caleb," the younger man replied.

Robbie closed the firebox door, then put down his coal shovel. He stepped over behind Caleb and squinted through the front window at the moonlit bridge ahead. He was about to walk toward the open rear platform when he was startled by the sound of crashing glass just behind where Caleb and he were standing. It sounded so much like a breaking bottle that he turned to chide the older man for smuggling whiskey on board and not sharing it.

Seeing Caleb's surprised expression, Robbie realized that the noise had some other source. As he started to look around, he smelled a curiously sweet and pungent odor and then felt a harsh, burning sensation in his nostrils and throat.

The young fireman started to open his mouth to speak, but his lips and tongue felt thick and unresponsive. He could see the engineer wavering on his feet, his eyelids fluttering and his eyes rolling back. Suddenly the older man sagged to his knees and then crumpled over on his side and lay motionless on the floor.

Bending down, Robbie reached toward him, but his own legs gave way, and he felt himself spinning dizzily through the air. He landed on something soft and had the fleeting thought that it was Caleb's belly. And then he sank deeper and deeper, until he was falling through a black, bottomless void.

Chapter 2

"NOW, THAT WASN'T SO BAD, WAS IT?" NORA SUTHERLAND asked as Jim Hart finished the last of his Delmonico steak.

"No . . . they certainly put on the dog for us tonight," Hart proclaimed, setting down his fork and knife and grinning at Nora, who laughed lightly.

"What's so funny?" a male voice asked, and Nora looked up to see Stuart Kennedy approaching through the dining car, which had emptied out considerably during the course of their dinner.

"Stuart, I'm glad you came. I'd like you to meet Jim Hart, a reporter with *The Rocky Mountain News*. Jim, this is my brother, Stuart Kennedy."

Hart stood and shook Kennedy's hand, then resumed his seat.

"Will you join us?" Nora asked.

Nodding, Kennedy reached for a chair from a neighboring vacant table. He was just pulling it over when the train whistle blasted and the dining car lurched abruptly, throwing him off balance. He grabbed hold of the chair and managed to stay on his feet. But then the car lurched again, this time more violently, as the brakes engaged and the wheels locked. Dishes went flying off the tables, and several passengers with their backs to the front of the car—Jim Hart included—were thrown backward over their seats. Kennedy held onto his chair, but it did not help, for he and the chair both went tumbling to the floor. Nora was thrown forward against the table, which was anchored to the floor and held her in place.

The screeching sound of locked wheels against metal rails filled the car, and sparks could be seen flashing past the dark windows as the entire train shuddered to a jerking halt. Then slowly the car settled back in place, the screeching replaced with the furious hiss of steam and the cries of the startled passengers, who lay sprawled across the tables and floor.

As Kennedy picked himself up, he realized that he had slid about ten feet down the aisle. Beside him, a portly woman was struggling to her knees, her hat askew but still pinned in place, her dress hiked up around her ample thighs. She whimpered more with fear and embarrassment than pain as Kennedy offered his hand and helped her to her feet.

As soon as the woman straightened her dress and regained some measure of decorum, Kennedy left her standing on tottering legs and went to check on Nora. Jim Hart was already on his feet and was helping Nora from the table. They stood looking around for a moment, assuring themselves that everyone in the car was all right.

"Do you always make an entrance like that?" Hart asked Kennedy, who grinned more from relief than from the humor of the comment. Around them, everyone began to speak excitedly and simultaneously, until the car was a babble of voices.

"Do you think we hit something?" Nora asked.

Shaking his head, Kennedy said, "I don't think there was a collision. Perhaps an obstruction on the track."

"Let's find out," Hart suggested, and the three of them started forward through the car, stepping carefully over broken dishes and spilled food.

Kennedy was the first out onto the vestibule between cars. Rather than passing through the forward door to the next car, he turned to the right side door and released the latch, swinging the door open. Then grabbing hold of the vertical rail beside the doorjamb, he stepped to the edge of the vestibule and leaned out from the car.

Looking ahead, Kennedy saw that the night sky was orange with sparks and flames and billowing with smoke. The tracks curved gently to the right, which allowed him to get a better view of the section of track in front of the train.

"There's a fire—just ahead of our train," he announced as Hart and Nora came up behind him. "I'll go see what it is."

"I'm coming, too," Hart said as Kennedy jumped to the ground.

"Help me down," Nora called as Hart leaped down beside Kennedy. Hart started to reach up to help her, but Kennedy who was a good half-foot taller, moved in front of him and caught Nora as she dropped from the vestibule.

"Go on ahead. I'll catch up to you," Nora told the two men as she hiked up the ankle-length skirt of her maroon dress and started awkwardly forward along the gravel roadbed.

"Are you sure?" Kennedy asked.

"Go on. They may need help."

Kennedy and Hart took off at a run. As they passed the two passenger cars ahead of the dining car, they were joined by other men who were climbing down and hurrying forward along the tracks.

"Know what it is, Jim?" one of the men called to Hart, who shrugged his shoulders.

"A train wreck!" someone else shouted from farther ahead.

As Kennedy and Hart neared the locomotive, they began to make out the scene on the track ahead. Indeed there had been some sort of a wreck involving a freight train. The train apparently had been heading south on the same track as their passenger train, for now the two men could clearly see the caboose some one hundred feet ahead of their locomotive. Beyond the caboose, several boxcars were derailed, with the fire concentrated around what appeared to be the locomotive and tender.

"Two trains," Kennedy suddenly blurted, grabbing Hart's arm and pointing toward the distant fire.

It took a moment for Hart to make anything out through the intense fire and smoke. And then he saw what Kennedy was indicating. There were two locomotives on fire, and beyond the second locomotive was another line of derailed boxcars.

"A head-on collision?" Hart mumbled, slowing to a walk.

"Looks like it."

The two men had just passed the front of their own locomotive, and Hart glanced to the far side of the train and saw the northbound rails. "But there are two sets of tracks here," he said to Kennedy. "How could the trains collide head-on?"

"Let's find out."

Moving to the flat roadbed between the two sets of tracks, they continued forward at a run, joined by the other reporters who had been in Cheyenne with Jim Hart. Reaching the caboose, which stood undamaged upon the rails, they hurried past it and began to circle the derailed boxcars. Many of the cars miraculously had sustained only minor damage, though a few were little more than splintered wood atop twisted-metal chassis.

The two men had to slow down as they approached the locomotives, which indeed had collided head-on and now were burning furiously. Amazingly the conflagration had not spread to the boxcars behind the locomotives, with the solid metal tenders having served as sort of a fire wall. The fire appeared to be dying out as it exhausted the supply of material in the exploded boilers. Apparently the coal in the tenders had not ignited, and there was a good chance the fire would play itself out in the next hour or so.

As more people began to gather on the tracks, Kennedy saw a pair of men standing not far away, each holding a lighted railroad lantern. Recognizing the taller man as the engineer of the passenger train and the younger one as his fireman, he prodded Hart and pointed at the crewmen, then headed over to where they were standing.

"Any idea what happened here?" Kennedy asked the tall, exceedingly gaunt engineer, whose face looked sheet white even in the warm glow of the fire.

Coming up alongside, Hart produced a small notebook and pencil and prepared to write.

"It's a hell of a mystery," the engineer muttered.

"What do you mean?"

"The northbound was on the wrong track. They must've seen each other coming around the bend but didn't have time to stop."

Other reporters began to gather around the train crew and fire questions at the engineer.

"Did you jump clear just before impact?" one man yelled, not realizing that the engineer was from the passenger train.

"Anyone killed?" another asked.

"Was it sabotage?"

"How'd they get on the same track?"

"Enough!" Kennedy shouted. "Let the man speak."

"I really don't know anything more than you," the engineer insisted. "Somehow the northbound was on the wrong track."

"But how?" someone asked.

"Maybe at the South Platte. The river's less than a mile ahead, and the northbound side's being rebuilt, so the trains use the same rails in both directions. Something must've gone wrong with the switching system, and the train wasn't shunted back onto its own track after crossing the bridge."

"Wouldn't they realize they were on the wrong track?"

"I don't know," the engineer replied, clearly uncomfortable with being under interrogation. "It's dark. They must not have seen—till it was too late."

"What's your name?" one of the reporters asked.

"My name?" the gaunt man said in surprise.

"Yes. For my story."

"Riley. Gene . . . uh, Eugene Riley."

"Is that R-e-i-l-l-y?" The reporter spelled it out as he wrote on a pad.

"No. Just R-i-l-e-y."

"Think anyone's alive?" Jim Hart asked, looking up from his own notepad.

"In there?" the engineer said incredulously, nodding toward the slowly subsiding inferno that had engulfed the two locomotives. "Not likely. You're welcome to go take a look," he added facetiously.

As the swarm of reporters continued to barrage the engineer with largely unanswerable questions about the crash, a woman called, "Stuart, over here!"

Kennedy and Hart turned to see Nora Sutherland on the far side of the derailed train, waving at them from between a detached pair of cars. The two men immediately crossed the tracks and scrambled between the cars to where she was standing with a man dressed like a farmer. Beside him was a buckboard wagon, while a bit farther down the track toward the rear of the train was another wagon with a pair of men on the seat.

"Mr. Price and a few others arrived on the scene shortly after the crash—about twenty minutes before we got here," Nora said as the two men came over. "They're from a small town nearby."

"It's called Evans," the farmer drawled. "Just a store

and a few houses near the river over yonder." He pointed vaguely to the southeast.

"Did you see the accident?" Hart asked.

"Nope. Some folks heard it, though, and then we seen the fire."

"Did you find any survivors?" Kennedy put in.

"Couldn't get near the locomotives. We checked the cabooses, but they was empty."

"Are you certain?" Kennedy said in surprise.

"I sure am," Price replied. "I checked 'em both myself."

"Is that unusual?" Hart asked, again jotting down notes in his pad.

"It certainly is," Kennedy proclaimed. "There is always a man in the caboose to keep an eye on the condition of the cars ahead and signal the engineer if there's a problem."

"Maybe the caboose men jumped clear before the crash," Hart suggested.

"Did you find anyone near the tracks?" Kennedy asked the farmer, who shook his head.

"Then maybe they were riding in the locomotives," Nora suggested. "Surely that must happen sometimes."

"Yes, it does," Kennedy admitted. "But it's clearly against railroad regulations. If one caboose was empty, I'd go along with that premise. But both? The odds are overwhelmingly against it."

"The odds are also against a head-on collision," Hart pointed out. "But it happened."

A couple of the other reporters, apparently realizing that the engineer and fireman did not have much more to offer them, headed over to see what Jim Hart was up to. Realizing that the buckboard wagons might mean that a town was in the area, one of them hurried over and asked, "Is there a telegraph office nearby?"

"Evans ain't got a telegraph," Price said, shaking his head. "But Greeley does."

"Where's Greeley?"

He pointed north along the tracks. "About five miles back up the line."

"Will you take us there?" the reporter asked.

"Now?" the man said dubiously.

"I'll give you five dollars."

As the farmer stood scratching his head, the rest of the reporters began wandering around the derailed cars in search of additional information for the stories they planned to write. Seeing the buckboards, they rushed en masse to where the farmer was standing and began pumping him for information.

Realizing that things were becoming a circus, Kennedy whispered something to Nora, and then she told Jim Hart that they were going to speak with the engineer again. Hart replied that he would join them in a few minutes and stood watching as they slipped away from the group and headed back to the other side of the train.

Slowly the herd of reporters pieced together the same information that Hart and the Faraday agents had just learned from the farmer: The cabooses were empty, and no survivors had been found. The general consensus was that the only people on the freight trains had been in the locomotives and that everyone had died in the fiery crash. Furthermore, the accident was the result of the failure—either mechanical or human—of the north-bound train to be shunted back onto its own track after crossing the South Platte River.

Deciding that they had more than enough information on which to base a story, the dozen or so reporters struck a deal with the wagon owners to take the entire group to Greeley, where they could telegraph their reports to their respective papers.

"Aren't you coming?" one of them asked Jim Hart as the reporters began to climb into the backs of the wagons.

Hart, who was standing near the front of the wagon speaking privately with the farmer, turned to his col-

league and replied, "I'm going to stick around for a
while. I want to check the locomotives once the fire dies
down."

"That could take hours," the reporter pointed out.
"You'll miss your deadline for the morning paper."

"I'll take my chances," Hart told them. "Go ahead."

As soon as the reporters were in place, seated precari-
ously in the two wagon beds, the drivers took up the reins
and turned their vehicles, heading north along the dirt
service road that ran alongside the tracks.

Jim Hart watched until the wagons had disappeared
into the night. Then he turned and headed back between
the derailed cars to where Stuart Kennedy and Nora
Sutherland were standing beside the engineer of the
passenger train. Kennedy was holding one of the lanterns
now, and the young fireman was nowhere in sight.

When Hart came up beside them, Nora asked what the
other reporters were doing, and Hart explained that they
had hired the farmers to drive them the few miles north
to Greeley so they could telegraph their stories to their
newspapers.

"Aren't you afraid of being beaten by the competition?" Nora asked.

"Let them fall over each other to get the story in first,"
Hart said in a slightly derisive tone. "They can have it
first. . . . I want it fullest. I'm willing to bet that there's
more to this story than what we've discovered so far."

"I agree," Kennedy put in. "I've just spoken to Riley,
here"—he nodded at the engineer— "and he's agreed to
hold the train while I check the shunting switches at the
bridge."

"Where would the train be going, anyway?" Hart
asked. "It certainly can't plow through this wreck and
continue on to Denver."

"But it can go in reverse—back up the line to Greeley."

"You mean those reporters didn't have to—?"

"Precisely."

Hart grinned. "Well, a madcap buckboard ride in the middle of the night will add a little atmosphere to their stories."

"You want to take the fireman with you?" the engineer asked Kennedy. "I sent him back to watch the train."

"I don't think that'll be necessary."

"But the two sides of the bridge are connected with a set of pneumatic switches, so that the lever on each side controls both switches," the engineer explained. "You'll need someone on this side to see that it works when you throw the lever on the far side. Maybe I'd better come with you and—"

"I'd like to go," Hart interjected.

"Yes, I think that's a good idea," Kennedy agreed. He turned to the engineer. "You should probably take the train up the line to Greeley and wire Denver to send up a repair crew to clear the tracks."

"What about the two of you?" Nora asked.

"Why don't you go along on the train and return with a wagon for us?" Kennedy suggested.

"I'll be back as soon as I can," she promised.

"We'd better be off then," Kennedy replied.

"Here, take this." Riley handed Hart the lantern. "There's plenty of light around here to guide the lady and me back to the train."

Kennedy embraced Nora, and then he and Hart started down the tracks beside the derailed cars. As they neared the still-burning locomotives, Hart came to a halt and stood looking at the aftermath of the inferno. He shook his head. "I don't think we'll be able to look around in there for a while."

"Even if we could, I'd bet everything would be consumed," Kennedy replied, stopping beside Hart.

"Still, there might be some evidence."

"That will have to wait for trained investigators."

"Tell me, Mr. Kennedy—"

"Stuart," Kennedy insisted.

Hart nodded. "Well, Stuart, may I ask what your

interest is in all this? If you don't mind my saying, it seems a bit unusual that a locomotive engineer would assist a passenger in launching a preliminary investigation like this."

"Is this on the record?" Kennedy glanced down at the notebook and pencil that protruded from Hart's breast pocket.

"Off the record—for now."

Kennedy started down the tracks again, with Hart walking beside him. As they passed the locomotives and continued alongside the second set of derailed boxcars, Kennedy said, "We never had time to be formally introduced. Did Nora tell you anything about me?"

"Just that she's your sister, and that you're on your way to Kansas City to visit relatives."

Kennedy nodded. "But did she tell you what I do—for a living, I mean?"

"I'm afraid not."

"I work for the Union Pacific Railroad," Kennedy said, using a cover that he and other Faraday agents regularly adopted. Since the Faraday agency often worked for the Union Pacific, arrangements had been made with the railroad to confirm the employment of a select list of Faraday agents, should inquiries be made.

"I usually work out of the Chicago office in the insurance division," Kennedy went on. "I'm the one who gets to send out insurance investigators after accidents like this, so this should be a good opportunity to remind myself what it's like in the field."

"Then why keep things off the record? Certainly having your name in the newspaper would make you look good with your superiors back at headquarters."

"I'd rather avoid publicity, for several reasons," Kennedy told him. "First, we like to keep these investigations as quiet as possible. There are a number of possibilities here, from human error to a mechanical breakdown to sabotage. The ultimate finding could have a major impact on any insurance settlement, so we'd like to do what we can to minimize outside pressure. And as for personal publicity, there's nothing I want less. Local insurance investigators will be assigned to the case, and I don't want them thinking I'm looking over their shoulders." Kennedy smiled ruefully at Hart. "Also, by keeping a low profile, I'll have the opportunity to see firsthand how our Denver office handles a case."

"Very smart," the reporter commented. "But this is a major news story. You can't expect me to—"

"I'll make you an offer," Kennedy interrupted. "Mention the insurance investigation, if you want. After all, that's standard policy. But keep my name out of it and also keep me informed of any new evidence you may turn up. In return, I'll make sure you get exclusive coverage of anything my office discovers."

"You'd do that?" Hart asked a bit skeptically.

"Why not. The rest of those reporters seem more concerned with getting the story first than with getting it right. You strike me as being more concerned with uncovering the truth, Jim . . . if I may call you that. And the truth is what we both are interested in."

"Stuart, you've got yourself a deal," Hart said with a grin as he stopped in place and shook Kennedy's hand.

Fifteen minutes later, Stuart Kennedy started alone across the bridge that traversed the South Platte River, leaving Jim Hart at the shunting switch on the north side. They had already determined that the north switching rails were not set to shunt the northbound train back onto its own track after crossing the bridge, which explained how it ended up on the southbound track. This still left open the question as to why the crew did not immediately realize the mistake, back the train up, and manually throw the switch to shunt them back onto their own track.

As Kennedy approached the south switching point, he assumed that he would find the rails set in a position to shunt the northbound train onto the single track. Most likely the pneumatic system had broken, so that the switch on the north side failed to be engaged automatically when the lever was thrown on the south side. But as he held the lantern over the switching rails, he was shocked to discover that the rails were in the wrong position. There were only two possible explanations. Either something mechanical had gone wrong, so that the switch reversed itself after the train was shunted onto the single track, or else someone had deliberately reversed the switch while the train was crossing the bridge.

Kennedy walked over to the lever that worked the switches. Raising the lantern, he swung it left and right to indicate to Hart that he was about to test it. After getting the return signal from Hart, he threw the lever and heard the switching rails reverse. A moment later Hart waved the lantern to signal that the rails had reversed on the north side, as well. Then Hart threw the north switch, and Kennedy confirmed that the south rails responded properly.

A few minutes later, Jim Hart crossed the bridge, and the two men discussed the situation. It was obvious that the switches were in perfect working order. That meant that after the train had been shunted onto the single track, something must have happened to reverse the switches.

"But if it was sabotage, why didn't the crew notice the mistake when their train failed to return to its own track?" Hart pointed out.

"Sabotage only makes sense if the crew was somehow unable to respond to the situation."

"Do you think they were . . .?"

"Killed? Before the crash?" Kennedy mused. "It's a possibility, but we may never know—not after that fire." Kennedy thought for a moment, then said, "There's still the possibility of a mechanical breakdown."

"What do you mean?"

"Sometimes these switches start acting up, and if the operator doesn't throw the lever all the way, it can temporarily engage and then slip out of position." Testing his theory, Kennedy walked over to the lever and threw it back and forth several times.

"You mean perhaps they threw the switch, but not quite all the way," Hart concluded. "Then after the train passed onto the single track, the lever slipped out of position and reversed the switches."

"It's possible, but unusual." Kennedy again tested the switch. "It feels solid, but a mechanic will have to check it out. Even if that proves to be the case, it doesn't explain why the crew didn't discover the mistake when they reached the other side."

"Perhaps they had been drinking," Hart suggested.

"I hope not—though it would certainly benefit the railroad."

"Why?" Hart asked.

"Human error. It's always better to blame it on the crew than the equipment. Personally, I find it distasteful —unless it really can be proved that the crew was at fault."

While Kennedy tested the switch a few more times, Hart held his lantern high and made a circle of the area, looking for any clue as to what might have happened when the northbound train passed through earlier that night.

After a few more minutes, Kennedy called over to him, "We'd best get going. It's too dark for any kind of thorough investigation, and Nora will be back with the wagon before long."

Hart had climbed down off the gravel roadbed and was standing near some brush beside the service road. When he did not respond, Kennedy took a few steps toward him and asked, "Are you ready to go?"

"Over here," Hart called, raising his lantern and looking up at Kennedy. "I think I may have found something."

As Kennedy approached and was about to scramble down off the roadbed, Hart waved for him to halt.

"Not there," he said excitedly. "Come down over there." He pointed to a place about twenty feet away.

Kennedy followed the younger man's unusual instructions and headed over to the place Hart indicated.

"Now stay off the dirt," Hart instructed as Kennedy approached. Again following directions, Kennedy kept to the grass between the gravel roadbed and the dirt service road.

"What have you found?" Kennedy asked as he came up beside Hart.

"I'm not sure. Look at this."

Hart lowered his lantern and held it over the soft earth. Kennedy immediately saw the numerous footprints that led down from the roadbed and then crossed the service road.

"And look over here."

Hart took Kennedy over to where he had almost come down off the roadbed. It was easy to see that the gravel had been disturbed, as if a number of people had clambered down the side.

"This could have been made by anyone," Kennedy pointed out. "A number of trains stop here each day."

"Yes, but look at this."

Hart led the way across the dirt road, following the trail of footprints into the brush. In a small clearing a few feet away were the hoofprints of a number of horses.

"Shall we follow them?" Hart suggested, pointing to where the hoofprints entered and departed the clearing along a narrow trail that led into the woods.

"It's pretty dark, but why not?" Kennedy agreed. "At least a short way."

With Hart in the lead, the two men started down the path. Kennedy held his lantern in his left hand, his right hand never far from the Smith & Wesson under his coat. They had gone only about a hundred yards when Kennedy grabbed Hart's sleeve and pulled him to a halt, signaling him to be quiet. The two men lowered their lanterns and stood listening for a moment, and then they heard what sounded like someone moaning.

"Hold this," Kennedy whispered, handing Hart his lantern. "And wait here."

Alone, Kennedy moved cautiously forward, trying to make out the narrow trail through the woods in the thin moonlight. As soon as he was far enough away so that Hart would not see, he slipped his revolver from the shoulder holster.

Ahead it seemed somewhat lighter, as if there was a gap in the trees. As he approached, he crouched down and began to move from tree to tree until he was at the very edge of a wide, grassy clearing. Hiding among the trees and brush bordering the clearing, he looked out and tried to discern the dark objects that dotted the landscape.

There came another moan from the left side of the clearing, and then one from just in front of him. Slowly Kennedy's eyes adjusted to the light, and he realized that what he was looking upon were six bodies that lay sprawled throughout the clearing. At least two were alive, and Kennedy decided to risk revealing himself.

Stepping out into the clearing, his revolver still at the ready, Kennedy approached the nearest body. It was a man who was moaning faintly, and as Kennedy knelt beside him, he saw that the man was dressed in the garb of a railroad engineer. Looking around, he saw that the others were dressed similarly.

Jumping to his feet and holstering his gun, Kennedy raced over to the trail and called for Jim Hart, who came at a run. Kennedy took back his lantern, and together the men examined the bodies. They discovered that all of the men were alive and that none had any noticeable injuries, such as bruises or gunshot wounds. Yet all six men were either unconscious or nearly so.

Stooping beside one of the moaning men, Kennedy set down the lantern and rolled the man onto his back. His eyelids were fluttering, and he began to groan louder. Kennedy gently patted his cheeks in an attempt to revive him.

"How is he?" Hart asked, kneeling beside them.

"I think he's coming around," Kennedy replied as he continued to pat the man's cheeks.

The man seemed to be struggling to open his eyes, and slowly he succeeded, at first for only a few seconds and then for increasing lengths of time, until at last he was able to look up at the two strangers hovering over him.

"Wha . . . what hap—?"

"Shhh," Kennedy soothed. "Rest easy. You were unconscious, and we found you here in the woods."

"Woods? B-but . . . the train . . ."

"Don't worry about that. Just lie back and rest for a few minutes."

"I can't," the man said in a surprisingly strong voice as he sought to get up.

Seeing the man's determination, Kennedy helped him to a sitting position.

Meanwhile, Jim Hart went over to one of the other men who had been moaning, and a minute later he called over to Kennedy, "This one's coming around, too."

"What happened?" the man seated with Kennedy asked.

"There was a collision. Were you on a northbound freight train?"

"No. We were heading south." He looked up at Kennedy in concern. "A collision?"

"Your train collided with another train head-on just north of the South Platte bridge."

"Head-on? But how?"

"The northbound was on the wrong track. Don't you remember any of it?"

The engineer sat straining to recall what had happened, then sadly shook his head. "Nothing. I . . . I must've passed out or something."

"Then how did you get here?" Kennedy asked.

"Where am I?"

"On the far side of the river, almost a mile south of the accident."

"I . . . I don't know." The man sat shaking his head in confusion. Looking around him, he saw that another man had been helped to a sitting position by the other stranger. He blinked his eyes to clear them, then declared, "That's Caleb Williamson. What's he doing here?"

Jim Hart was speaking quietly with the man named Caleb. He looked over at Kennedy and said, "This one was the engineer on the northbound."

"How'd he get here?" the first engineer asked in surprise.

"The same way you did," Kennedy replied. "Someone carried you here."

"But why?"

"That's what we aim to find out."

Fifteen minutes later, all six crewmen—the engineer, fireman, and caboose man for each train—had been revived. When Kennedy and Hart questioned them, they all gave the same puzzling story: As they had neared the South Platte River, they each had experienced the same dizzying sensation and then had passed out. The locomotive crew of the northbound train thought they remembered slowing down as they approached the bridge, but the fireman had no memory of having left the train and thrown the switch. Two of the men—a caboose man on the southbound and the fireman on the northbound—recalled smelling an unusual odor just before passing out. The caboose man said it was sweet and cloying, while the fireman was certain it was pungent and burning. That was the last memory any of them had before awakening in the forest clearing.

As soon as the crewmen had recovered enough to walk without assistance, Kennedy and Hart led them back along the trail to the train tracks. Along the way,

Kennedy pointed out the hoofprints and asked if anyone recalled seeing horses. No one did.

Kennedy, Hart, and the six crewmen made their way up onto the roadbed of the Union Pacific tracks and started the trek north across the river, eventually coming to the site of the train wreck. The fires had died out in the locomotives, and they were able to give a cursory examination inside the cabs. There was no evidence of another person's having been on board, though the heat had been so intense that it would have obliterated most anything or anyone inside.

A few minutes later, Nora Sutherland came riding up in a buckboard wagon drawn by a team of two horses. She had rented it from one of the Evans farmers, who decided to spend the night in Greeley. She was shocked to see the missing crewmen, and Kennedy quickly filled her in on discovering the men lying unconscious in the woods not far from the bridge.

The crewmen climbed into the wagon bed, while Nora, Kennedy, and Hart shared the front seat, with Kennedy driving the team. As they headed north to Greeley, Nora described with some amusement how the passenger train, traveling in reverse, had passed the two wagons of reporters and had beaten them to Greeley. By the time the wagons arrived in town, the engineer had already telegraphed a full account of the collision to Denver and had been told that a repair crew would be sent out as soon as it could be organized. The passengers would have to spend the night in the single inadequate hotel or aboard the train, which probably could resume the journey sometime late the next morning, after the tracks had been cleared.

It was well after midnight when the rented wagon arrived in Greeley, which was little more than a single street with a few houses and stores. Kennedy pulled up beside the passenger train, which had backed onto a siding at the station, and the crewmen piled out. Leaving them to have a reunion with the surprised crew of the passenger train, Nora led Kennedy and Hart to the small telegraph office down the street.

The two men expected the place to be filled with reporters and a buzz of activity, and they were surprised to find it occupied only by the elderly telegrapher, who was busy tapping away at the key. He looked up briefly as the trio entered, and then he resumed his work.

"Where are the others?" Hart asked. When the man did not reply, he added, "The reporters . . . where have they gone?"

"Denver," the old man muttered.

"But the tracks are out."

"Didn't take the train. They left me with these"—he held up a stack of papers—"and hired themselves a couple of coaches to race them down to Denver. Expect they'll be there by sunrise." He paused, then commented, "Those boys don't seem to care how much money they spend, do they?"

"Damn!" Hart blurted. "They'll get there hours ahead of me."

"You one of them?" the telegrapher asked.

"A reporter? Yes."

"You'll have to hurry if you're gonna catch up with them."

Suddenly Hart began to grin, and then he shook his head and laughed aloud. "Let them go," he declared. "I don't need to beat them there."

"What do you mean?" Nora asked.

"They all filed their bulletins, and now they're hurrying home to complete their stories. Some of them will probably come back up by train in the morning to get a revised account for the next day's paper. Meanwhile, they've rushed off without the most important part of the story—and I'm the only one who's got it."

"The train crews," Nora said.

"Exactly. I can send the entire story by wire to my own paper, and we'll be the only one to have it in the morning."

"Train crews?" the telegrapher asked.

"Yes," Kennedy put in. "Mr. Hart, here, found them lying unconscious in the woods not far from the site of the crash."

"I'll be damned!" the old man exclaimed. "Should I stop sending these, then?" He lifted the stack of papers left by the reporters.

"No, you go right ahead."

"But they're wrong. They all say the crewmen were killed in the crash."

"Never you mind," Hart told him with a smile. "Those reporters paid you good money to have their bulletins transmitted by wire, and you've an obligation to send them as written. But as soon as you're done, I'll have a more complete story for you."

"Whatever you say." The telegrapher turned back to the key and resumed tapping out the messages.

"I'd better get to work," Hart told Kennedy and Nora. He pointed at a desk against one wall. "I'll be over there writing my own story, if you need me."

"Remember what we discussed," Kennedy said quietly. "I'd rather not—"

"Don't worry," Hart interrupted. "You won't be mentioned anywhere in the story."

"Thank you," Kennedy replied. Taking Nora by the arm, he added, "We'll be resting on the train."

"And Jim," Nora put in. "Congratulations."

"Hold those congratulations until tomorrow morning when we're certain I'm the only one with the true story."

"You will be," she assured him.

"Which reminds me . . ." Hart turned to Kennedy. "Is there any way you can delay reporting the discovery of the crewmen to the authorities in Denver?"

"What do you mean?"

"If they find out too soon, the other papers may get the information before they go to press."

"How much time do you need?" Kennedy asked.

"Let's see . . ." He glanced at the wall clock. "It's

almost one. Four hours would be plenty. By then all the papers will have been put to bed.''

Kennedy nodded. "I think I can arrange that for you, seeing as how you were the one to find them. I ought to question the crewmen again, anyway—after they've had some rest, of course. I'll just wait to make my report to Denver until that's finished—about five o'clock or so.''

"Thanks.''

"I'd like to ask a favor in return, however," Kennedy added.

"What kind?''

Lowering his voice so that the telegrapher would not hear, Kennedy said, "It regards those reports by two of the crewmen of smelling something unusual just prior to passing out. That's the only lead we have right now, and I was hoping you'd agree to not reporting it yet—at least until we get a chance to pursue it.''

"Agreed.''

"Good," Kennedy replied. "I said we could help each other, didn't I? Now sit down at that desk over there and write yourself a story that will be the talk of Denver.''

"Denver?" Hart said almost derisively. "This story is going to find its way to the front pages of every newspaper from San Francisco to New York.''

Chapter 3

A REPAIR CREW OF THE UNION PACIFIC RAILROAD WORKED through the night to clear the obstructed rails near the South Platte River. Though their work would take a number of days to complete, the southbound track was sufficiently clear to allow traffic to pass by late the next morning. The first train down the line was the passenger train from Cheyenne and points west, which had spent the night on a siding at Greeley.

At ten minutes past twelve that afternoon, the train pulled into Denver, Colorado, almost twelve hours behind schedule. Jim Hart was seated with Stuart Kennedy and Nora Sutherland in their private compartment, and as he looked out the window at the station, he was not surprised to see a knot of reporters on hand. After all, *The Rocky Mountain News* would have been on the stands for several hours by now with the exclusive report of the discovery of the missing crewmen from the two demolished trains. Every other paper would be scrambling to get the full story in time for the evening edition.

Even as the train was coming to a halt, a teenage boy who had leaped aboard went rushing into one of the second-class cars with an armload of newspapers. Waving one aloft, he shouted, "Read all about the great train wreck!"

Even though the passengers had seen the accident firsthand, they rushed to buy up the copies, as if they could not be certain the incident had occurred until they read about it in the paper.

In first class, Stuart Kennedy was opening the door of the private compartment when the newsboy entered the car and started down the aisle. Signaling that he wanted a copy, Kennedy reached into his pocket, took out a coin, and gave it to the boy.

"You shouldn't have wasted your money," Jim Hart told Kennedy as the boy handed him the paper and disappeared down the aisle. "That's the *Post*. For the full story you'll have to read *The Rocky Mountain News*."

"Let's see what they've got," Kennedy said, unfolding the paper.

Kennedy turned the newspaper so that the others could read the banner headline, which proclaimed: *Trains Collide Head-on In Mystery Crash*. A smaller subhead declared: *Both Crews Missing; Feared Lost In Fiery Inferno*.

"Fantastic," Hart muttered, relishing his success in scooping the competition.

"Let's go," Kennedy said, reaching up to the rack above one of the seats and pulling down a large carpetbag and a somewhat smaller leather valise.

Jim Hart pulled down his own travel bag, then offered Nora his arm. With Kennedy leading the way, the trio moved out of the compartment and down the aisle to the vestibule. A porter was on hand to take the group's luggage and usher them through the crowd that was gathered in the station.

"Dougherty!" Hart called as he stepped down onto the platform. "Over here!"

Nora and Kennedy looked in the direction Hart was waving and saw a middle-aged, disheveled-looking man with salt-and-pepper hair and a walrus mustache. Though it was impossible to see the man's mouth under his mustache, it was clear that he was frowning.

"What is it?" Hart asked, sensing Dougherty's mood as the older man pushed his way through the crush of people and approached.

"This," Dougherty grunted. There was a newspaper under his arm, and he unfolded it and held it aloft for Hart to see. It was a copy of *The Rocky Mountain News*, and it bore a set of headlines almost identical to the ones in the *Denver Post*.

Flabbergasted, Hart grabbed the paper from Dougherty and examined it more closely. The lead story bore Hart's byline, but it made no mention of his discovery of the missing crewmen.

"What the hell happened?" Hart demanded. "This isn't what I telegraphed!"

"I know," Dougherty said, glancing briefly at Nora and Kennedy, as if wondering whether it was all right to speak in front of them. Apparently deciding in the affirmative, he continued, "That ass of a managing editor yanked the lead off your story."

"Blaine?"

"Who else? Mr. Timothy 'Self-Righteous' Blaine himself. Said your story was preposterous and checked with a friend of his at the *Post*. When it turned out they didn't have your lead—and nobody else did, as well—he decided it was some kind of a hoax."

"That bas—" Hart caught himself and just muttered under his breath.

"Well, when word came in this morning that you were right, all *hell* broke loose. . . . Uh, excuse me, ma'am," Dougherty added, looking sheepishly at Nora, who waved off his concern. Turning back to Hart, he went on, "By then the paper was on the streets. We won't have the up-to-date story until this afternoon's edition."

"Along with everyone else," Hart grumbled. He looked toward the rear of the train, where the crewmen from the wrecked trains had just emerged from the caboose. As if a starting gun had gone off, the assembled reporters raced through the crowd and surrounded the men, shouting questions and falling over one another in a mad effort to get the latest piece of information for the afternoon editions of their newspapers.

"I'm sorry." Dougherty shrugged his shoulders. "I tried to convince Blaine to trust you, but you know what he can be like."

"I've been with *The Rocky Mountain News* for less than a year, and already I've had my fill of that man." Shaking his head, Hart started across the platform and into the station, with Dougherty and the two Faraday agents following. As he entered the lobby, he came to an abrupt halt. "I *have* had enough," he declared. "I'm going to quit and—"

"You don't have to," Dougherty interjected. "He's gone."

"Who? Blaine?"

"Yes—fired. He got the boot just as soon as the publisher found out how badly he botched up this whole affair." For the first time, Dougherty allowed himself a smile. "I don't have to tell you what a celebration that set off."

Hart placed a hand on the older man's shoulder and gave him a warm smile. "I appreciate your telling me. But I've made up my mind."

"But you don't have to quit now," Dougherty argued. "You can—"

"Yes, I do. And not just because of what happened with this story. Timothy Blaine may be gone, but someone just like him will take his place. I'm tired of answering to men who can think of nothing better for me to do than to cover silly town meetings and barn dances. I want to call my own shots—make my own mistakes."

"But what will you do?"

"First I'm going to write a detailed account of that wreck and how I found those crewmen, and I'm going to sell it to the eastern press. Though it's no longer an exclusive, it will be the most complete and accurate account. Then I'm going to find out what made those trains collide."

"Why not do that for *The Rocky Mountain News*?" Dougherty urged.

"I want to do it my way." Hart held out his hand.

"I suppose I understand," Dougherty said, shaking Hart's hand. "Perhaps if I was younger I'd do the same thing."

"Thanks, Dougherty."

"Now, don't be a stranger, young fellow."

"I won't." Hart paused, then added, "Tell the office I'll be by tomorrow to pick up my things."

"Sure thing." Dougherty nodded at Nora and Kennedy, then turned to leave.

"One other thing," Hart called after him. "Also tell them that they'd do well to make you managing editor."

"Me?" Dougherty laughed gruffly. "I'm afraid I'll have to be content to finish my career covering those silly town meetings and barn dances. They've already appointed a new managing editor."

"Don't tell me. It's Willoughby," Hart guessed, and Dougherty nodded. "The publisher's nephew," Hart said by way of explanation to Nora and Kennedy. "I figured as much. As I said, if it's not Timothy Blaine, it's someone just as incompetent."

With a grin, Dougherty clapped Hart on the back. "You've made the right choice, son. Get out while you're young, and don't sell yourself short. Those eastern papers have got plenty of money. Make sure they pay you up front—and by the word."

"And through the nose," Hart declared.

"Always through the nose," Dougherty said with a laugh as he turned and walked away.

For a few moments, Hart and the Faraday agents stood

in silence, and then Nora commented, "It's a shame things didn't work out the way you'd hoped."

"It's probably for the best. I'd been considering striking out on my own but hadn't worked up the courage. Now the decision has been made."

"Will it be difficult making a go of it working as a free lance for papers back east?" Kennedy asked.

"I don't think so. The West is too big for most eastern newspapers to send out their own correspondents, so they end up buying their stories from papers out here after the stories have already run. If I can give them the story faster as a special correspondent, they don't have to credit another paper and can gain some prestige for themselves. And if the news stories are slow in coming, I can always augment them with magazine features."

"It sounds reasonable," Kennedy replied.

"And I've got the first story all ready to go—I just have to rewrite it and telegraph it out. Then I'll have a better idea how my new venture will go."

"I hope it works out for you," Nora put in.

"Enough of this talk," Hart said. "Since you've decided not to rush off to Kansas City, I'm sure you'll be wanting to settle in at one of the city hotels."

"Yes, we would. Do you have any recommendations?" Kennedy asked.

"The Orient Hotel. It's not the biggest, but it's the cleanest and most convenient."

"If you think so."

"I ought to. It's where I maintain a room myself."

"Then shall we go?" Kennedy suggested. He signaled the porter, who was waiting off to the side with the luggage. Giving the man some coins, he asked that the bags be brought to the Orient. Then he turned, waved his arm toward the exit doors, and said, "If you'll show us the way . . ."

"I'd be delighted," Hart replied, holding out his right arm to Nora.

Taking hold of it with her left, she slipped her right

hand through Kennedy's arm. Then the trio headed through the station and out into the brisk but sunny September afternoon.

After unpacking his valise in his third-floor room at the Orient Hotel, Stuart Kennedy knocked on the connecting door to the adjoining room. A moment later it opened, and Nora invited him in. She was still unpacking her carpetbag and looked surprised to see him dressed to go out.

"I'll be finished soon," she told him.

"No need to hurry," he replied as he sat down on the edge of the bed. "I thought I'd go over to the telegraph office and fill Matthew Faraday in on the latest events. Then I'd like to pursue one of the leads—provided Mr. Faraday tells us we're on the case."

"Which lead? The gas smell?" she asked as she removed a long green gown from the bag and brought it over to hang in the wardrobe.

"Yes. A crewman from each of the trains reported an unusual odor just before passing out. They described it somewhat differently, and actually only the fireman on the northbound said he believed it was a gas of some kind. It's not much, but it's the one thing that links the events on both trains."

"What do you think it might have been?"

"I don't know, but I intend to find out. It's true that we didn't turn up any new evidence when we reexamined the cabooses and burned-out locomotives before leaving Greeley this morning. Still, I'm convinced those crewmen were not imagining things."

"You know what some people are saying, don't you?" Nora commented.

"I know: The wreck was due to human error, and the crewmen jumped clear just in time and then pretended to pass out just to protect the guilty parties."

"What do you think?"

"I don't accept it."

"Neither do I," she admitted, coming over to the bed and sitting beside Kennedy. "Making up a story about passing out and then being spirited off the train would have required all six crewmen to have jumped from the trains safely before the crash. Then the two guilty men in the northbound locomotive would have had to convince the four innocent people to go along with it. That's far too risky—and ridiculous. But just for the sake of argument, let's pretend that they did jump clear at the last second."

"All right." Kennedy nodded. "But the rest of the theory immediately starts unraveling. Just put yourself in their position. If you wanted to cover up your own responsibility, would you make up such an outlandish story and go so far as to wander off into the woods and pretend to be unconscious?"

"I doubt it."

"Of course not. The easiest thing to do would be to go back to the bridge and cut the pneumatic line, so that the switching lever on one side would fail to throw the switch on the other side. Then you'd only have to explain why you didn't notice that the train failed to return to its own track—a minor infraction at best."

"You're right," Nora agreed.

"That still leaves one problem," Kennedy said somberly.

"Which is?"

"Why the hell someone would gas the crewmen on two trains, remove them to a place of safety, and then set the trains on a collision course."

"We can be sure of two things," Nora pointed out. "Someone wanted those trains destroyed, and they didn't want anyone hurt in the process."

"And something else," Kennedy added. "Whoever is responsible had to have a lot of help in order to carry off the scheme with two trains simultaneously."

"An inside job?" Nora suggested. "Perhaps someone disgruntled with the railroad?"

"Most likely—unless they were after something aboard one or both of the trains. We'll have a better idea later today, when a final determination is made whether anything was stolen."

Kennedy stood and walked toward the door to the hall. "I should be back in a couple of hours," he told her.

"Are you sure you don't want me to come along?"

"It would be best if you waited here—perhaps down in the lobby. That young Mr. Hart seems to have taken a liking to you, and it wouldn't hurt—"

"I thought that's what you had in mind," she said with a rueful smile.

"It doesn't hurt to encourage the friendship . . . just so long as it doesn't get out of hand. A reporter can be very useful; he has contacts it would take us months to establish. And if he turns up any new evidence, I want to be sure that we're the first to learn of it."

"He seems like such a nice, dedicated man. I'd hate for us to use him just to—"

"We're not using him," Kennedy insisted. "Consider it mutual assistance. If he continues to help us out, I'll make sure that he's on the inside when we bring this case to a close."

"I suppose I can't tell him we work for Faraday," she said somewhat dishearteningly.

"What do you think?"

"I know I can't." She frowned. "It rubs me the wrong way, that's all."

"It's better for all of us—Jim Hart included—if he goes on thinking I'm handling an insurance investigation for the railroad and you're nothing more than my sister."

"I know. That doesn't mean I have to enjoy it."

"You also don't have to enjoy yourself when you're spending time with that young reporter." Kennedy narrowed one eye meaningfully, then turned the doorknob and started to push open the door.

"Is that a touch of jealousy I detect?" Nora stood and approached Kennedy at the open door.

"Of that little fellow?" He waved off the notion as ridiculous. "He's friendly enough but not your type."

"And what is my type?" she asked coyly.

"Oh, someone about six feet tall, blue eyes, sandy-blond hair, devastatingly handsome . . ."

With a playful smirk, Nora pushed Kennedy out into the hall, saying, "If you come upon anyone who looks like that, don't hesitate to bring him on by." She closed the door behind him and leaned back against it, shaking her head and grinning.

At the telegraph office, Stuart Kennedy met privately with the manager and presented authorization papers from Western Union that allowed him to operate the equipment personally, an arrangement worked out between the Faraday Security Service and Western Union. The manager then stepped out of his office and told the young key operator that Kennedy was on hand to examine the equipment for the home office and that the operator should take a fifteen-minute break and get some fresh air.

As soon as the young man had departed, Kennedy sat down at the equipment and began sending the transmission codes that would patch him through directly to the telegraph operator at Faraday headquarters in Kansas City. Since the manager had returned to his private office and no one else was on hand, Kennedy decided against sending the entire message in a secret code, since that would require time for decoding at the other end. Instead, he used Morse code to report the events of the previous day and request instructions as to how he and Nora should proceed.

There was a short delay while Matthew Faraday himself was summoned. Faraday informed Kennedy that he already had been gathering whatever information was available on the collision and had been in communication with top officials of the Union Pacific Railroad. Kennedy and Nora should continue to use their standard cover and pursue whatever leads they had. However, the railroad company had not yet determined that the incident was anything more than a case of negligence that was being covered up by the crewmen, and therefore the Faraday agency was not officially on the case. Still, the Union Pacific officials had agreed to give the Faraday agents full authority to carry out a preliminary investigation.

When Kennedy detailed the reports of a strange-smelling gas and said that he would first pursue that angle, Matthew Faraday suggested that Kennedy see if a chemist named Harold Trimm still ran a pharmacy in Denver. Trimm's uncle and Faraday were longtime friends, though they had not seen each other in several years. The uncle used to brag about his nephew's budding career as a research chemist, carried out in the rather extensive laboratory he maintained at the rear of his pharmacy. Perhaps this Harold Trimm, if he was still in Denver, could help Kennedy and Nora determine the nature of the alleged gas.

Kennedy signed off his transmission only moments before the key operator returned. After assuring the young man that the equipment was in proper working order, Kennedy thanked the office manager and left.

Back on the street, the Faraday agent hailed a gurney cab and asked the driver if he knew of a pharmacy run by a man named Harold Trimm. When the man had confirmed that there was a druggist by that name who had an establishment on Larimer Street, Kennedy climbed into the back of the cab and directed the driver to take him there.

As the cab drove along the wide boulevards of Denver, Kennedy marveled at the changes that had come over the city. He had been a mere lad of fifteen when his father first brought him to Denver some nineteen years before, in the summer of 1870. Then Denver had been little more than a trading town for the growing Colorado mining regions and had been home to less than five thousand residents—still, a bustling community for the West at that time. Yet no one would have guessed the growth that was to come with the arrival of the railroads. By 1880 the population had jumped to more than thirty thousand, and the city had begun to boast all the trappings of civilization: citywide gas lighting, an elaborate network of streetcars, even a fledgling telephone system. The following decade had been one of such unparalleled growth that the upcoming 1890 census was expected to push Denver's population well over the hundred-thousand mark.

As Kennedy watched the parade of carriages and trolleys, horsemen and pedestrians, he shook his head in wonderment at what was emerging from the wild West. The ladies were as fashionably dressed as any Boston society matron, and the gentlemen's eastern-style suits were cut from the finest imported cloth. Most striking of all was the total absence of firearms, and he suddenly felt self-conscious about the Smith & Wesson that bulged under his own western-cut suit jacket. Yet he knew that this prosperous city, though it worked so hard at emulating its larger sister cities of the East, was not so far removed from its rugged western roots. There might no longer be an open display of weaponry, but guns were always close at hand, either under carriage seats or hidden in the pockets of those expensively tailored clothes.

Kennedy was shaken out of his reverie as the gurney came to a halt in front of a building in the Larimer Street business district. As he climbed down from the cab, he looked over the storefront and read the ornately lettered sign: *H. Trimm, Druggist.* Turning back to the gurney, he paid the cabbie the fare and entered the pharmacy.

The shop appeared to be small but prosperous, with a variety of health-related general goods on shelves along the left-hand wall. The opposite wall was lined with shelves of pharmaceutical ingredients, in front of which sat a long counter topped with an ornate brass cash register and a row of bottles filled with mint sticks and penny candies. Just now the only person in the store was an affable-looking man with thinning brown hair and a ready smile, whom Kennedy took to be in his early thirties.

As Kennedy approached the counter, the fellow looked up from the pill machine in front of him, arched his eyebrows, and asked, "May I be of service?"

"Harold Trimm?"

"Yes. Have we met?"

"No. I work for the Union Pacific Railroad. My name is Stuart Kennedy."

"What can I do for you?" Trimm inquired with an attentive smile.

"I'm investigating that train collision last night. It was reported—"

"What a terrible tragedy," Trimm cut in, shaking his head. "It's fortunate no one was hurt. But it's strange how those crewmen turned up the way they did."

"You've heard about that?"

"Why, yes. I haven't seen the evening paper yet, but in a pharmacy, one tends to hear the news as soon as it hits the streets."

"That's what I've come about," Kennedy told him.

"Those crewmen?" Trimm asked in surprise.

"Yes. You see, I'm investigating the case for the railroad, and—"

"But how can *I* be of help?"

"Can I speak to you confidentially?"

Laying his palms flat on the counter, Trimm stood a bit straighter. "I am a pharmacist," he intoned almost religiously. "Like a doctor, everything we say will be kept in the strictest of confidence."

"Good," Kennedy declared, trying not to smile. "You see, there's one fact that will not be reported in the newspapers, and it's important to our investigation that it not become a matter of public record—just in case a crime was involved. For now, it's our only lead."

"Whatever is it?" Trimm said, his eyebrows arching impatiently.

"Gas," Kennedy said flatly. "More precisely, a peculiar odor that a couple of crewmen claimed to smell just before they lost consciousness."

"You think it was a gas?"

"That's why I've come to you. I've been told you are the leading research chemist west of Chicago."

Trimm took a deep breath, puffing himself up with importance. "I've had a modicum of success in the field of chemistry," he said with unconvincing modesty.

"Then you're the man to help me find out whether that smell was some kind of gas that knocked out those men—and whether the gas was of a natural cause or . . ."

"The result of foul play," Trimm said ominously.

"Precisely."

Trimm looked around cautiously, as if confirming the obvious fact that the store was devoid of customers. Then lowering his voice to a conspiratorial whisper, he said, "Perhaps you should come back here." He beckoned with his forefinger as he walked to the end of the counter, opened a door in the back corner of the store, and passed through to the room beyond.

Kennedy followed along his side of the counter, pausing for a moment at the open doorway and peering across the threshold.

"Come in," Trimm insisted, waving Kennedy into the spacious back room, which was flooded with light from a bank of windows along the far wall and from a large skylight in the center of the high tin ceiling. A pair of long worktables stood beneath the windows on either side of a door that led to the back alley, while the side walls were covered floor to ceiling with shelves of supplies.

"My laboratory," Trimm declared, standing in the center of the room and sweeping his arm in a wide arc to take in the worktables, covered with test tubes, beakers,

and other apparatus, and the shelves of bottles, each
labeled with the appropriate chemical formula.

"Quite impressive," Kennedy commented, nodding.

Trimm crossed to a rolltop desk beside the door they
had just passed through. Sitting down in the swivel chair,
he took a writing tablet from one of the drawers, picked
up a pencil, and said, "Can you describe the smell in
more detail? You say it was gaseous?"

"The fireman on one of the locomotives said so. He
described it as a pungent gas that burned at his nostrils
and throat. One of the caboose men just mentioned
smelling something sweet and cloying."

"Hmm." Trimm shook his head as he busily took
notes. Glancing up momentarily, he asked, "The others
didn't report any unusual odors?"

"No. But they were all quite disoriented, and I
wouldn't trust their memories."

"Just as you cannot trust the memories of the two who
claimed to smell something unusual. That could be little
more than a hallucination accompanying the state of
unconsciousness."

"Though that wouldn't explain how they passed out in
the first place," Kennedy pointed out.

"No, I suppose not," Trimm agreed. Looking down at
the paper on which he was writing, he shook his head. "A
real mystery, we've got here."

"And one we'd like to solve as quickly and quietly as
possible."

"You can rely on my discretion, Mr. Kennedy."

"Thank you." Kennedy waited for a moment as
Trimm scribbled more notes, which from a distance
appeared to be a series of chemical formulas. "Do you
have an idea what it could be?" he asked presently.

Trimm turned in the swivel chair and faced Kennedy.
"It could be quite a number of things. I'd like to run a
couple of tests before I come to any preliminary conclu-
sions."

"I understand. Perhaps if I came back tomorrow?"

"Splendid." Trimm rose from the chair. "Or I could send word if I find out anything," he suggested.

"I'm staying at the Orient Hotel on—"

"I've been there many times."

"Thank you for all your help," Kennedy said, backing toward the door to the main room.

"Oh, Mr. Kennedy . . . would you do me a favor?"

"What is it?"

"On your way out, could you turn the sign on the front door to *Closed* and lock the door behind you?"

"Yes, of course."

Harold Trimm smiled and immediately crossed to one of the shelving units. He ran his forefinger across the labels on the bottles, stopping every now and then to take down a bottle and place it on the nearest worktable.

Standing in the doorway, Kennedy stared at him for a moment, then turned and walked back through the pharmacy. He found it easy to surmise that Trimm handled his duties as a druggist only grudgingly. It was when he was back in his laboratory, huddled over the beakers and Bunsen burners, that he was truly in his element.

"Elements," Kennedy corrected himself with a smile as he opened the front door, reversed the sign, turned the lock, and pulled the door shut behind him.

Nora Sutherland reached up to knock on the door of Jim Hart's room on the second floor of the Orient Hotel, and then she hesitated and pulled back her hand. Drawing in a calming breath, she told herself that all she was doing was pursuing a friendship—one that could be mutually beneficial. Yet she knew that Hart's interest in her could easily go beyond friendship, and she did not like the idea of doing anything that might lead him on. She especially hated lying to him by claiming to be nothing more than the sister of a Union Pacific insurance investigator. But her role as a Faraday agent often required her to use deceit in order to ferret out the truth. She only hoped that when this whole affair was over, Jim Hart would understand and forgive her.

Taking another deep breath and holding it, Nora knocked on the door. She exhaled slowly as a man called, "Yes? Who is it?"

"Nora Sutherland," she replied, her voice betraying none of her trepidation. She looked down to make certain that her white evening shawl was in place over her blue satin gown, then reached up to pat her long brunette hair, pulled into a chignon at the back of her neck.

There was a brief pause, and then the door swung open to reveal the young reporter, who was still dressed in his brown suit but without the jacket. "To what do I owe this pleasure?" he asked, beaming with delight.

"I hope you don't think me too terribly bold," she began, "but my brother's work apparently has kept him late at the railroad offices, and I was hoping you might be available to escort me to dinner."

Nora inwardly cringed at telling the small falsehood. In truth, Stuart Kennedy had recently returned from his visits to the telegraph office and pharmacy but had encouraged Nora to dine alone with Jim Hart.

"I can think of no better delight," Hart declared. "Just let me get my jacket."

Leaving the door open, he disappeared across the room, returning a moment later with the jacket over his arm. He stepped out into the hall and closed the door behind him, locking it with a key.

"Is my tie straight?" he asked as he turned to Nora.

"Just about." Nora reached out and adjusted the two sides of the bowtie. As she did so, she felt his warm brown eyes staring intently at hers. She felt a bit disconcerted, a feeling that was augmented somewhat by their being the same height, putting their eyes at the same level.

"Thank you," he said as she let go and took his arm. He led the way down the hall.

After coming down the wide central staircase into the main lobby, Jim Hart suggested they dine at a restaurant just a few buildings down the street rather than at the hotel dining room. Nora readily assented, and they headed out into the surprisingly warm evening air.

The couple had only gone half a block when behind them a booming voice called, "Hart! Jimmy Hart!"

Nora felt Hart's arm stiffen, as if he recognized that voice and was not at all pleased to hear it.

"Hold up, Jimmy boy!" the voice declared.

Nora noted that the voice was slurred, and as she and Hart turned around, she was not surprised to see that the man who had called out was tottering slightly as he came down the street. He was a tall man and was probably once thin but had gone slightly to paunch. His glazed eyes were small and dark and were set close beside a long, aquiline nose. His black hair was not very long, but it was quite disheveled, and though he did not sport a beard or mustache, he apparently had not shaved that morning. Still, he was no derelict. His suit was of the finest cut, and despite being tipsy, he carried himself with the air of a gentleman.

"Been waitin' for you," the man said, his head cocked slightly as he stumbled up to them. He raised a big, bony hand and waved it toward Nora. "Who's she?" he asked abruptly.

"None of your business, Blaine," Hart replied testily.

"Mr. Blaine t'you," the man shot back.

"If you'll excuse us," Hart said with what passed for politeness. He started to turn away, but Blaine reached out and grabbed his jacket sleeve.

"Not so quick. I want a few words with you."

"There's nothing to be said between us." Hart pulled his sleeve free but did not turn away.

"I think there is." Blaine stood tottering on unsteady

legs, staring back and forth at Hart and Nora. "Know what your gentleman friend did?" he finally asked, not waiting for a reply. "He got me fired, is what."

"I did nothing of the kind. Your own stupidity caused that."

"Watch your tongue, boy," Blaine shot back. Turning to Nora, he grinned smugly and went on, "It's my fault, everyone says. Should've run the story, no matter how ridiculous it sounded, they say. Even if it came from this wet-behind-the-ears, sorry excuse for a newsman."

"Come along," Hart said, taking Nora's hand and starting to turn away.

"Just a minute!" Blaine railed, grabbing Hart's sleeve again and jerking him around. "I dunno what your game is, Jimmy boy, but I'm gonna find out! Ever since you came to *The Rocky Mountain News,* you've been makin' the rest of us look foolish with your exclusive stories, one after another. Now they say if I don't convince you t'come back, I can forget about comin' back myself." Blaine turned and spat at the sidewalk. "Well, I'll be damned if I grovel to the likes of you!"

"You're damned already," Hart muttered.

"You little bastard!" Blaine cursed. Without warning, he swung his arm and backhanded Hart across the face, stunning him. Letting go of the smaller man's sleeve, Blaine grasped his collar and twisted it savagely as he yanked him up onto his toes.

"I'm onto you!" he shouted, this time swinging a fist that connected with the tip of Hart's chin. The young reporter's legs crumpled beneath him, and he would have sagged to the ground had it not been for the bigger man's iron grip on his collar.

It was when the drunken man pulled back his fist to lash out for the third time that Nora stepped in. She acted coolly and efficiently, chopping down with the side of her open, rigid right hand against the inner elbow of the arm that was holding Hart's collar.

With a cry of surprise and pain, Blaine released his grip, allowing Hart to drop to his knees, and spun toward Nora.

Standing her ground, Nora drew her right arm across her chest and swung it in a wide arc. This time the edge of her hand connected with the tall man's neck, staggering him and almost knocking him off his feet.

For a moment Blaine stood bent over, his hands against his knees as he gasped for air. Then like a wild, wounded bear, he raised up, let out a gagging roar, and came at Nora with both fists flailing, totally unconcerned that she was a woman.

Nora planted her feet firmly and threw up first her right, then her left arm to ward off the flurry of blows directed at her by the enraged man. When his punches struck nothing but air, he backed up slightly to redirect his aim. Nora took advantage of his hesitation and moved in, crouching down slightly and throwing a solid punch to the big man's midsection. As he doubled over, she stepped forward and drew up her knee, striking his nose. There was the sickening crack of broken bone as the force of the blow threw him backward off his feet and onto the ground, where he lay holding his nose and moaning piteously.

Jim Hart was just rising from his knees now, and Nora helped him to his feet. He looked dazed, though his shock was more from having seen Nora in action than from the beating he had taken.

"Wh-where did you . . . ?" His voice trailed off in wonderment.

"Learn to fight?" she said, stalling as she tried to think up a believable answer.

"You were . . . unbelievable," he commented, somewhat disconcerted.

"My father was once a prizefighter. He taught Stuart all his tricks. I guess I picked it up by watching."

As Nora helped Hart brush himself off, they noticed that a small crowd had gathered during the fight, which had ended so quickly that none of the male spectators had had a chance to intervene. Just as one of the men was telling the couple that the marshal had been summoned, a man wearing a badge pushed his way through the crowd. He was tall and muscular, with a drooping mustache and black hair that had begun to gray at the temples.

The lawman quickly determined that the man on the ground was Timothy Blaine, the former managing editor of *The Rocky Mountain News,* and that he had instigated the fight. Introducing himself as Marshal Sam Novak, the lawman directed two of the spectators to pick up the semi-conscious man and haul him off to jail.

"That won't be necessary," Jim Hart put in, his voice weak and woozy as he rubbed the spot on his chin where he had been struck.

"I think it is," Novak declared as the two spectators hoisted Blaine to his feet.

"But I don't want to press charges," Hart told him.

"Nor do I," Nora added.

"That's your decision," Novak said, "though I think it's the wrong one."

"He was drinking, that's all," Hart said. "I think he'll cool down when he sobers up."

"And he'll do that sobering up in jail." Novak nodded, signaling the two men to drag Blaine away, and then he turned back to Hart. "It's up to you whether or not you press charges for assault, but I intend to lock him up anyway for public drunkenness and disturbing the peace. The judge will probably give him a two- or three-day sentence, and then if you still don't want to press charges, I'll let him go."

Novak started to walk away, then turned back and said, "If I were you folks, I'd seriously consider pursuing the assault charge. My experience is that a thing like this doesn't go away all that simply."

"We'll consider it," Nora assured him. She took hold of Jim Hart's arm to steady him as the marshal walked away and the crowd dispersed. When they were at last alone, she turned to him and asked, "Are you still hungry?"

With a sheepish grin, he said, "Believe it or not, I think I'm hungrier now than I was before."

"Then let's try out that restaurant of yours." Smiling, she led him down the street.

Chapter 4

"HEY, JULES! WAKE UP!" THE DRIFTER CALLED IN A HARSH, guttural whisper as he shook his partner's shoulder with one hand while clutching a lit, stubby candle in the other. The man was short, thin, and exceedingly homely, his bony face a stretched mask of pockmarks and dirt-encrusted creases. His friend was equally gaunt, but even curled up on the straw-covered floor of the empty boxcar, it was plain to see that he was a good foot taller and far more agreeable looking, if not handsome.

"Jules!" the little man called louder, above the din of the moving freight train. "Get up! We're stopping!"

There was a low, mournful moan, and then Jules rolled over onto his back and forced open his pale, bloodshot eyes. "Wha' the hell?" he blurted, blinking his eyes against the flickering light of the candle. "Lemme sleep, Smitty."

"We're stopping!" Smitty repeated, his voice edged with concern. "Listen."

Waving Smitty back, Jules turned his head and pressed

his ear against the floor of the boxcar. He only had to listen for a moment to realize that his little friend was right and that the train was coming to a halt.

"It ain't light out yet," Smitty said agitatedly as Jules stretched and pushed himself up to a sitting position. "We can't be in Denver."

"Maybe we're stopping to take on water."

"I don't like it," Smitty whined as he rose and backed against one of the closed sliding doors, where he stood wringing his hands together. "Maybe we oughta get off. They catch us in here, they'll want the full fare, and we don't got enough between us for a watered-down whiskey in a whorehouse."

"Nobody's gonna make you pay nothing, boy, so don't wet your pants," Jules chided as he pulled himself to his feet and reached all the way up to the roof, stretching his spine and yawning. "They'll probably shoot you, of course, but they won't make you pay."

"I don't like it one bit," Smitty repeated, shaking his head slowly and deliberately.

"Get away from there," Jules ordered, approaching the door and waving Smitty away. "Lemme take a look." He pulled a revolver from behind his belt and held it pointed toward the ceiling.

"Be careful. Don't let 'em see you," Smitty cautioned, slipping a long-bladed knife from his own belt as he backed toward the far end of the boxcar.

"Just shut up and blow that thing out."

As Smitty blew out the candle flame, Jules grabbed hold of the handle at the edge of the door and gave a hard yank to the left. With a loud rasp, the door slid open a couple of inches.

Jules pressed his face against the opening and looked out at the landscape for a moment. It was somewhat lighter outside, with the prairie bathed in the cool, blue light of a harvest moon.

"Don't see nothing," he said as he again grasped the

handle and pulled the door open wide enough to push his shoulders through.

Smitty hesitantly approached the open doorway. "What is it?" he asked as his tall friend leaned out through the opening and stared toward the front of the train, which was quickly coming to a halt now in a squeal of brakes and grinding metal.

"Lights ahead. Looks like lanterns."

"Damn. Must be the Denver rail yard."

"It ain't Denver," Jules called back. "We're out in the middle of the prairie."

"What is it, then? A station?"

"Don't think so. Appears to be a track crew." As the freight train came to a final halt, Jules leaned back slightly so that only his head stuck out of the boxcar. "Yep, that's what it is. Looks like they've been laying rails between the two tracks."

"What for?" Smitty asked in a nervous whisper.

"How the hell do I know?" his friend said in exasperation. "Maybe the westbound track's out ahead and we're being put onto the eastbound for a ways."

Suddenly the train began to move again. Jules jumped back from the doorway when he heard the clanging as first the forward car and then each successive car was jerked into motion by the one ahead of it. The noise grew increasingly loud until what sounded like a sharp thunderclap struck their own car, and it lurched forward. Then the banging quickly receded into the distance as the remaining cars rolled into motion.

The train moved forward at a crawl. Jules risked looking out the doorway a final time as their boxcar approached the place where a dozen lanterns illuminated a gang of railroad men, who stood on the opposite track watching the freight train pass.

"Get back!" Jules whispered as he moved away from the doorway and retreated into the shadows. He and Smitty stood side by side, gun and knife in hand as they peered across the car and through the partly open door. A moment later they saw the lanterns and caught a glimpse of passing faces, and then Smitty momentarily grabbed the bigger man's arm as the train lurched to the left and was shunted onto the eastbound track.

The boxcar straightened out as it proceeded slowly down the eastbound rails. Only the thin moonlight could be seen outside, and Jules hazarded another look through the door, first looking toward the rear of the car and then ahead toward the locomotive.

"That's what it is," he said, leaning back in and pushing closed the door. "We've been put on the east-bound track, is all. We'll probably be shunted back somewhere down the line."

There was the sharp scratch of a match being lit, and then the flickering glow of the stubby candle again filled the car.

"Why don't you get some sleep?" Jules asked as he tucked his gun back behind his belt and lay on the floor.

"I . . . I don't feel like it," Smitty said, sitting down against the wall opposite the door they had opened. He cupped the little candle in his hands and stared nervously into the flame.

"Well, just keep quiet, then." Jules rolled over so that his back was to the candlelight.

"Sure thing, Jules," his little partner said softly, his wavering tone betraying his fear.

Smitty rested the candle on the floor in front of him and leaned toward it. With a slight shudder, he reached a forefinger into the hot, melted wax that was pooling around the burning wick. Withdrawing his finger, he held it close in front of his eyes, watching as the wax cooled and hardened into a creamy white shell.

Unbeknownst to the drifters, someone outside had seen Jules leaning out of the partly open boxcar door. It was a burly, black-haired man seated on horseback, who had taken up a position some hundred yards ahead of the track crew. He had been almost abreast of the boxcar when Jules first opened the door, and he had followed the car at a walk, watching as the tall, lanky drifter looked out upon the crew.

The big horseman made a mental note of which boxcar the drifter was in, then waited until that car had passed the track crew and had been shunted onto the eastbound rails. Cautiously spurring his horse forward, the man approached a buckboard that stood off to the side of the roadbed. A kerosene lantern was hanging from a pole at the rear of the driver's seat, casting enough yellow light to illuminate the wagon bed.

Pulling his horse to a halt at the rear of the wagon, the man reached down from the saddle to an open wooden crate that was filled with straw. Pulling aside some of the straw, he felt around underneath until his hand grasped hold of a fragile glass bottle, which he carefully lifted from the crate.

The man held the bottle up to the buckboard lantern. It was a conical flask with a narrow neck stoppered with a rubber cork, and it was filled to the base of the neck with a colorless liquid. He swirled the liquid slowly, his mouth quirking into a smile.

Cradling the bottle in his lap, the man kneed his mount forward. As he came up to where the work crew was watching the freight train pass from one track to the other, he called, "As soon as it's on the eastbound track, rip these rails up and put them back the way they were."

"Sure thing, McNally," one of the men on the ground called back with a wave. "We know what to do."

"Make sure there's no sign that these rails were ever connected," he added, kneeing the horse forward along-side the slow-moving train.

McNally carefully cushioned the bottle as he urged the horse to a trot. He passed the cars one by one until he drew abreast of the boxcar in which he had seen the drifter looking out. The door was closed now as he paced the horse to the speed of the train. Expertly guiding the animal with his knees, he dropped the reins, transferred the bottle to his left hand, reached to the left side of the door with his free hand, and grabbed hold of one of the rungs of the ladder that led to the roof of the boxcar. Slipping his right boot from the stirrup, he stepped onto the ladder and then swung his other leg over the saddle.

McNally stood on the ladder with his right arm hooked around one of the rungs as his horse peeled away from the train and dropped back. Still holding the bottle in his left hand, he hooked that arm around a rung and then let go of the ladder with his right hand and reached over to the handle of the sliding door. He gave it a hard push, forcing the door open about a foot or so. He caught a glimpse of candlelight as he grabbed the fragile bottle with his right hand and tossed it in a high arc into the middle of the boxcar.

There was a sharp cry from inside the car as the glass shattered. McNally immediately yanked the door closed and held it tight as he leaned away from the ladder and took a few deep breaths of the cool predawn air. He began to count out loud: "One, one thousand, two, one thousand, three, one thousand, four, one thousand . . ."

By the time McNally counted to one hundred, the train had come to a halt, indicating that all the cars had been shunted onto the eastbound track. He took a deep breath, held it, and pushed the door open wide. He held his breath as long as he could, making certain that the gas had dissipated before he cautiously let out a gust of breath and inhaled.

McNally smelled only the faintest trace of the sweet, pungent odor as he climbed into the car, which was still illuminated by a candle that sat burning on the floor. Beside it, a thin little man lay unconscious. Several feet away lay another man, equally thin but a full head taller. After checking to make certain that both men were fully overcome by the gas, he looked at the pile of broken glass in the middle of the floor. There was no sign of the liquid—not even a wet spot on the floor. The entire contents had been quickly transformed into a noxious gas upon contact with the air.

After picking up the pieces of broken glass and throwing them outside the boxcar, McNally stepped up to the tall man and nudged him with a heavy work boot, rolling him onto his back. Behind the man's belt was a revolver. He did the same with the smaller man and discovered a long-bladed knife.

McNally ran his hand through his greasy, short black hair as he stood staring at the two men, debating what to do. From their threadbare, dirty clothes and general unkempt appearance, it was obvious that they were nothing more than a pair of drifters who had boarded the empty boxcar for a free ride.

"Sorry, boys," he muttered as he bent down and took the knife and revolver from the two men.

Leaving the gun lying on the floor, McNally knelt beside the tall man and raised the knife in both hands. He drew in a breath, held it, and plunged the knife full hilt into the man's chest. He backed away as blood first spurted and then began to flow in rhythmic pulses from the fatal wound. The man's breathing slowed, and then his chest stopped rising and falling. Never once did he stir as he drifted into death, looking as tranquil as he had while unconscious.

Picking up the gun, McNally moved over to the smaller man and jammed the muzzle into his belly, angling it upward into the chest cavity. He pulled the trigger, and there was a muffled report. The body shuddered once from the impact of the bullet, then lay as still and peaceful as the other man.

McNally crossed back to the first dead man and pried open the fingers of his right hand. He forced the man's forefinger into the trigger guard of the gun and left the hand lying across his body with the gun dangling from it. Then he grabbed hold of the knife handle and jerked the blade out of the man's chest. Returning to the body of the little man, he placed the knife in the man's hand and rolled his body over on top of it so that it would hold the knife in place.

As McNally stood away from the bodies, he untied the bandanna from around his neck and wiped his bloody hands. He looked down at the bodies, pleased at his handiwork, then walked up to the candle and stomped on it, snuffing out the flame. Tossing the bandanna onto the floor, he walked to the open door of the boxcar and dropped down to the ground.

Seeing his horse standing nearby, McNally walked over to it and vaulted into the saddle. He took up the reins, kicked the horse into a gallop, and rode up to the locomotive. Quickly dismounting, he climbed into the cab and nodded at the man behind the throttle.

"Everything go all right?" he asked, glancing down at a pair of bodies lying on the floor of the cab.

The man at the controls turned and nodded. "Had no trouble with them two." He indicated the engineer and fireman on the floor. "Just tossed down the bottle from up there"—he nodded toward the roof of the tender behind the locomotive—" and waited a couple minutes, like you said. They passed out and fell right away, and I 'spect they'll sleep like lambs for a couple hours at least, just like them other ones did."

"You're sure they didn't get hurt when they fell?"

"Checked 'em twice," the man assured him.

"And you're positive they didn't see our men tearing up the tracks?"

"They was out cold two miles the other side of the shunt."

"Good. Remember, I don't want these men hurt. You know what to do now, don't you?" he asked, and without waiting for the man's reply, he continued, "Just drive this train another five miles west until you cross the bridge at Box Elder Creek. Benny will be waiting there with some extra horses. The two of you will carry these crewmen down to the riverbank and leave them lying there." McNally was interrupted by the arrival of a man on horseback.

"I got the caboose man here, boss," the man called, pulling to a halt beside the locomotive. There was a body slung over the front of the man's saddle.

McNally stepped to the back of the cab and helped the other man transfer the limp body of the caboose man to the locomotive. As the horseman rode off, McNally dragged the unconscious man into the cab and left him lying with the other two crewmen.

Catching his breath, McNally resumed his instructions: "As soon as the crew's down by the river, get back on board and blast your whistle three times—two shorts and a long. If everything went as planned, the eastbound freighter will be waiting a couple of miles to the west with Blackmun at the controls and Turner in the caboose. When you hear the return signal, start her moving, open the throttle wide, and jump clear. Then you and Benny go get Blackmun and Turner and ride back to the hideout. You got it?"

"Don't worry, Alvin. I'll get the job done."

McNally grinned. "I'm counting on you." He clapped the other man on the shoulder.

"I suggest you get off this locomotive of mine," the man at the controls said as he started to open up the throttle. "I've got another train to meet." He looked back at McNally and smiled broadly.

"Just make sure you and these sleeping gents over here aren't on the train when they do."

Alvin McNally walked to the rear of the cab and jumped down from the slowly moving train. He headed over to where his horse was waiting and climbed up into the saddle, then rode back toward the lights where the rest of his men were returning the tracks to their original condition.

As McNally approached the place where his men were working on the tracks, he noticed a one-horse buggy that had pulled up in the field halfway between the roadbed and the carriage road, which paralleled the tracks about one hundred yards away. Angling his horse toward it, he rode up to the buggy and glanced inside. In the growing light of dawn, he saw a little gray-haired man with a white mustache, dressed impeccably in a striped gray suit.

Leaning forward in his seat, the older man held forth a packet. "Go on, take it," he said in a gruff, cracking voice as McNally moved his horse up beside the buggy. "Ten thousand dollars, as agreed."

"I didn't expect to see you out here," McNally said as he took the proffered packet and stuffed it behind his belt. "I figured you'd come to the hideout, like last time."

The old man gazed over at the crew, which was busy tearing up the rails that had been laid between the two tracks. "This one was tricky," the man said. "I wanted to see for myself how you handled it."

McNally turned in the saddle and pointed toward where his men were working. "It was simple. We raised sections of both tracks and angled them in toward each other on temporary ties I stole from the rail yard where I've been working. Then we joined the tracks in the middle. It was a crude connection, but it was good enough to bring the westbound train across at a walk to the eastbound track. Now we're putting the rails back the way they were."

"What about the other train?"

"That was easy, since it's staying on the same track. A couple of my men slipped on board and knocked out the caboose man and locomotive crew, then took over the train. It's waiting on the other side of the Box Elder for the westbound train to get there."

"And the crewmen?" the elderly man asked, his voice edged with concern.

"We've followed your instructions. They'll be taken off the trains near the crash site."

"You're certain no one was hurt?" the man pressed, narrowing his eyes as he stared up at the big man on horseback.

McNally hesitated as a fleeting image of the dead men in the boxcar passed in front of his eyes. He knew that they would be found in the wreckage; however, it most likely would be assumed they got into some kind of an argument and killed each other prior to the crash. And with them dead, there would be no witnesses to attest to the work McNally's gang had carried out tonight.

McNally decided that there was no point in jeopardizing the lucrative funds they had been receiving from this mysterious unnamed gentleman, who thought nothing of hiring them to destroy these trains yet insisted that no one be injured in the process. "No one was hurt," he declared emphatically, meeting the older man's penetrating gaze.

"Good," the man said, settling back in his seat.

"Have you picked the time and place for the next collision?" McNally asked.

"Not yet. I'll send you word. In the meantime, you'd best keep working at the Denver rail yard."

"I don't like working there," McNally muttered.

"But it's come in handy," the old man said. "You wouldn't have known how to set this thing up if you hadn't."

"I'll be glad when it's over."

"It will be . . . soon enough."

McNally eyed him suspiciously. "Won't there be another—?"

"Yes. One more, at least. But that may be all."

"We'll be ready," McNally assured him.

"I know that you will," the man replied. With a nod,

he took up the reins and slapped them against the horse's back, turning the buggy around and driving back across the field to the carriage road.

Alvin McNally sat on his horse and watched as the buggy turned west toward Denver and disappeared into the dusty grayness. He shook his head as he wondered why that old man wanted to destroy these Union Pacific trains yet was so insistent that no one be hurt, going so far as to provide those curious bottles filled with that powerful chemical.

"Who cares," he muttered to himself with a shrug.

Glancing to the east, McNally saw that the sky was brightening. It soon would be daylight, and his men had not yet finished with their work. Slapping the reins, he rode toward them at a gallop, smiling to himself as he envisioned the trains that soon would be hurtling toward oblivion upon a single, unyielding track.

As the buggy raced west along the dirt carriage road, Edward Trenary thought of his meeting with Alvin McNally. He neither liked nor trusted the man, yet he had no choice but to use him. Only McNally commanded a gang sufficiently large to pull off a caper of this sort.

"One more time," he told himself with a smile. "After tonight, one more should be enough."

Ahead he could see the small twin bridges that traversed Box Elder Creek, the left one for road traffic, the right for trains. He did not see the Denver-bound freight train anywhere near the bridge, which could mean only one thing. . . . .

Trenary's thought was confirmed by a sudden, thunderous explosion a mile or so down the track. There were a number of smaller explosions, and then a brilliant flash of light that lit the morning sky.

Edward Trenary fought the reins to steady his skittish horse. As soon as the animal settled down, he urged it to a gallop and continued down the road. He wanted to see the wreck up close while the flames were at their peak. And then he had to put a good fifteen miles behind him so that he could be in Denver when word arrived of this latest mysterious tragedy.

As Trenary slapped the reins, the buggy jounced wildly down the rutted dirt road. To the east, dawn bathed the sky in a warm wash of oranges and pinks. To the west, the sky was already burning with a deadly crimson light.

Chapter 5

STUART KENNEDY AND NORA SUTHERLAND WERE HAVING A late breakfast in the dining room of the Orient Hotel when Jim Hart came rushing in. He looked around quickly, saw where they were seated, and hurried over to their table.

"What is it?" Nora asked in concern.

"Didn't you hear?"

"No. What?"

"There's been another crash."

"You're not serious!" Kennedy declared, sweeping his napkin from his lap and dropping it onto the table.

"Fifteen miles or so to the east on the Kansas Pacific branch, just this side of Box Elder Creek. Didn't the railroad send word to you?" Hart sounded a bit surprised that Kennedy had not been informed of the incident.

"They certainly should have," Kennedy replied, though in truth he had no such arrangement, since to this point he and Nora were working on their own in this case. "Were two trains involved again?"

"Just like before." Hart pulled out a chair and dropped onto it. "A pair of freight trains struck head-on. This time it was the westbound that somehow ended up on the eastbound tracks."

"Was anyone hurt?" Nora asked.

"Apparently not. As a matter of fact, by the time another train came upon the scene of the accident, the two crews had already regained consciousness near the scene and were wandering around a bit disoriented." Hart rose and pushed the chair back under the table. "I've rented a carriage, and I'm heading out there right now. Would either of you like to come along?"

"Why, thank you, we would." Kennedy pushed back his chair. "I'll just get our coats from upstairs." He turned to Nora. "Is there anything else you'd like?"

"I'll come up with you." She smiled at Hart. "We'll only be a moment, Jim."

"I'll be out front in the carriage," he told them as they headed from the dining room.

Fifteen minutes later, the two Faraday agents were seated beside Jim Hart as he drove the two-horse phaeton east out of the city. The day was sunny and mild, and at Nora's urging, Kennedy lowered the leather canopy as they rode along.

"Do you have any more details of the accident?" Kennedy asked as they left the city behind.

"Not really. I'm afraid I was one of the last to find out."

"What do you mean?" Nora asked from her place on the center of the seat between the two men.

"I no longer work for *The Rocky Mountain News,* so there was no one to contact me when the first report came in earlier this morning. Some of my friends should have told me, but they didn't. I suppose they remembered my firsthand account of finding the crewmen after the last accident and decided to keep a step ahead of me."

"So other reporters are heading out to the site?" Kennedy asked.

"They should already be there by now. As soon as I heard about the crash, I checked at the station and found out that a group of them had just left on a special train sent out by the Union Pacific to clear the tracks."

"How did you find out, anyway?"

"One of my reporter *friends* must have had a guilty conscience. He waited until the special train was leaving, then hired a boy to bring a message to me at the hotel—too late for me to catch the train, of course. He's probably out there now, feeling self-righteous about having informed me but secretly gloating that I'll be left with the table scrapings by the time I arrive on the scene."

"Being first is not always the key to success. You proved that at the last crash," Nora pointed out.

"I know. Which is precisely why I invited the two of you along."

"I thought it was because you liked us," Nora chided playfully.

"Are you joking? I'm a newsman, remember. We're not supposed to like anybody." He feigned a frown. "No, the truth is that your brother is my insurance policy."

"Insurance?" Kennedy said questioningly.

"You're an insurance investigator, right? That means you know the kinds of things to look for in a situation like this. And if you turn up any important evidence, I want to be at your side." He slapped the reins to quicken the pace of the horses. "I may not be first with the story, but I intend to be the most thorough. That's why I don't really mind missing that train."

"What do you mean?" Nora asked.

"The rest of those reporters will be rushed straight to the crash site. They'll have some time to look around and maybe even take a few photographs. Then they'll be whisked back in time to make their evening editions. We, on the other hand, will be able to take our time, go where we want, speak to whomever we please. Then I'll have all evening to send the most up-to-date report to the morning papers back east."

As the phaeton left Denver behind, Jim Hart tried to learn more about the background of his companions. Nora and Kennedy were understandably hesitant to say too much about their past, and they did their best to change the topic to the business of journalism and how Hart got started in his career. The young reporter seemed far more eager to discuss the future than the past, and he shared his dreams and aspirations with them. He had always seen his job with *The Rocky Mountain News* as a stepping stone to a larger career as a roving author and journalist who traveled the world in search of strange and exciting stories to send back to the American public, he explained.

"Another Henry Stanley in search of the elusive David Livingstone, I presume?" Nora asked.

Hart grinned. "I'll settle for unlocking the mysteries surrounding these train wrecks."

"If you do that, you should be able to write your own ticket with the eastern press," Kennedy commented.

"For a while," Hart agreed. "Unfortunately, in this business you're only as good as your last story."

Hart and his companions spent the next couple of hours in pleasant conversation as they followed the dirt carriage road that paralleled the railroad tracks. It was just after noon when they caught their first glimpse of the wreck, which had occurred in the middle of a broad meadow in the high grasslands of eastern Colorado. As in the first collision, the locomotives had been all but consumed in an explosive inferno, and numerous boxcars had been derailed, with some of them having caught fire and burned down to their chassis.

A small train, containing three flatcars and two passenger cars, waited on the tracks on the Denver side of the crash. In front of the train was a flatcar-mounted crane, which had been pushed to the site to help clear the tracks. At the rear of the train, the caboose had been replaced with a second locomotive, so that the train could return on the same track without having to run in reverse the entire way. Smoke billowed from the stack of the rear rather than forward locomotive; it was apparent that the train was preparing to head back to Denver.

Jim Hart turned the carriage off the road and headed across the field toward the train tracks. As they neared the crash site, he saw that a conductor was waving the crowd of reporters back to the waiting train. He steered toward a red-haired reporter who was standing alone and pulled to a halt in front of him.

"Jim, you made it!" the man called as he recognized the driver of the carriage. "I expected to see you on the train."

"I found out about it too late," Hart replied.

"That's right." The man masked a smile. "You're on your own now, aren't you? No editor to keep track of things and send you out on assignments."

"And that's the way I like it, Mike."

"Then you'll especially like this story. It's got all the elements for those Johnny-come-lately papers back east." He raised a hand, mapping out the words in the air as he intoned, "Explosions . . . destruction . . . death . . ."

"Someone died?" Kennedy interjected.

"Two people," the reporter said matter-of-factly.

Hart looked at him curiously. "I was told that the crewmen—"

"Not the crew. Two drifters were found in one of the empty boxcars of the westbound." He paused, then added, "I should let you get the details yourself, Jim, but never say Mike Spayne isn't a friend. . . ." He glanced back at the splintered wood and twisted metal of the derailed cars. "The fact of the matter is, those drifters weren't killed in that crash," he declared, his tone dripping with import. "They were dead already."

"Are you sure?" Hart asked.

"*Dead* sure. One took a bullet to the stomach, the other a knife to the chest."

"Maybe whoever caused the crash—" Nora started to say, but the reporter raised his hand and shook his head.

"I really shouldn't be handing everything to your friend on a silver platter, but I don't want you thinking we're all cutthroats in this business, so I'll tell you this much more: They weren't murdered; they killed each other. The weapons were found right there in their hands. Must've had a disagreement about whose boxcar it was."

The reporter looked over and saw that most of his colleagues were nearly at the train, which was ready to pull out.

"I've got to be going," he said. Smiling at Nora, he added, "You take good care of my friend Jim, now." Then he turned and walked away.

The last couple of reporters—one of them carrying a bulky dry-plate camera on a tripod—were walking away from the crash site as Jim Hart drove the carriage closer and pulled it to a halt. As they climbed out, Stuart Kennedy pointed to the train that had brought the reporters. It had been decoupled between the passenger cars and flatcars, and the rear engine and the passenger cars were beginning to pull away, leaving behind the other engine and flatcars to take the work crew back to Denver once the tracks were cleared.

As the train slowly started to move, the straggling reporters had to run to catch up. They leaped aboard the rear vestibule barely in time and only just managed to get the camera aboard in one piece.

Kennedy and Hart headed over to where the crew was working at clearing the rails. The cars that had not derailed or been damaged too severely would be pulled to Denver for repairs, while the ones that were beyond repair would be hoisted off the tracks with the flatcar-mounted crane and left lying beside the roadway until they could be broken up and removed.

Searching out the crew foreman, Kennedy and Hart questioned him about details of the accident and learned that it was remarkably similar to the one near the South Platte River, with one important difference. While the earlier accident occurred near a bridge where trains headed in both directions shared a single track, this crash had occurred along a stretch of tracks with no connecting rails. The only place the westbound train could have transferred tracks was at the last station to the east, and officials there had already confirmed that the train had been on the proper track when it passed through. It was a complete mystery as to how the train could have gotten onto the wrong track.

While the two men spoke with the foreman, Nora Sutherland opened a carry bag she had brought along and removed a small black box, approximately six inches long, three inches wide, and four inches high. There was a round opening at one end, centered in which was a small, recessed window. It was one of the innovative new hand cameras, called detective cameras because their size allowed them to be used surreptitiously.

Walking away from the carriage, Nora took a position some distance from the wreck and stood with her feet firmly planted a foot or so apart. Holding the camera waist high with the opening facing forward, she aimed it at the trains and then pressed a little button on the left side of the box. There was a click as a shutter opened and closed behind the recessed lens, and the picture was taken.

Nora turned a crank at the top of the camera to advance the roll of film. Then she walked closer to one of the burned-out locomotives and took another exposure. Again advancing the film, she proceeded to walk around the crash site and take numerous shots of the damage and of the crewmen at work.

As she made her way back alongside the westbound freight train, she saw a pair of men working between the last derailed boxcar and the first one that had managed to stay on the tracks. They had removed their shirts and were struggling with crowbars to detach the two cars, so that the derailed one could be removed from the tracks and the rest of the train hooked up with the locomotive that had been sent out from Denver.

Nora was intrigued by the image of the workmen and thought that it would make a good picture, especially since the man perched atop the coupler was slim and sinewy while the one on the ground was big and burly, with greasy black hair that shined as brightly as the sweaty sheen on his muscular body.

Hoping to catch them in a candid pose, Nora slowly raised the camera and took careful aim. She snapped the shutter just as the big man was turning in her direction. He did not seem to realize what she was doing but frowned at her anyway.

"Mind if I take your picture?" she called as she approached, hoping to add a posed shot to the candid one.

"That doesn't look like no camera," the big man grunted.

"Well, it is. And I'd like to take a picture of you boys with it."

"What for?" the slim man asked eagerly.

"The newspaper, perhaps," she replied.

The big man turned his back on Nora. "Don't want my picture taken," he grumbled.

"Come on," the other one said. "We could be famous." He grinned in anticipation.

"We don't even have our shirts on."

"Who cares. We'll look like prizefighters."

"Not me." The big man stooped down and slipped under the coupler, emerging on the far side.

"You can take one of me," the thinner man said, dropping to the ground and posing with his crowbar.

"Wouldn't you also be willing—?" Nora started to ask the big man, but he walked away and disappeared around the end of the car.

Shrugging, Nora aimed her camera at the more oblig-ing man and told him to hold steady. He gave what he thought was a suitably serious expression, and she clicked the shutter.

"That's all there is to it," she said, lowering the camera. "What's your name, in case we need it for a caption."

"Roger Mills," he said with enthusiasm. "Sorry about Vinnie," he added.

"Vinnie?"

He pointed over his shoulder in the direction the big man had wandered. "I don't know his last name. He's new at the rail yard, and a strange one—moody and all. But he's all right, I suppose."

"Some folks just don't like having their picture taken. They think it captures their soul." She grinned.

Roger chuckled. "I don't have to worry. I sold mine to the railroad ages ago."

"Thanks, Roger."

"Maybe you can try again when Vinnie comes back," he suggested as Nora started to turn away.

"I don't need to," she said, looking back at him. Lowering her voice, she added, "Just between you and me, I already took a good picture of Vinnie when you two were working."

"He didn't see?" Roger slapped his leg in amusement.

"It's all right. I'm sure he's got plenty of soul to spare." She thanked him again and then walked away.

Roger stood watching as Nora made her way back along the train. Suddenly the deep voice of the man named Vinnie interrupted his reverie.

"Let's get back to work," he thundered as he leaned over the coupler and prepared to attack it with his crowbar.

Roger turned to look at him and could not stop himself from chuckling.

"What's so funny?" the big man asked.

"Nothing." Roger laughed even louder.

"Come on. Out with it," the other man demanded, raising his crowbar menacingly.

"I was just imagining the look on your face when you see your picture in the paper."

"What are you talking about?"

"That pretty lady took your picture when you weren't looking."

"Are you sure?"

"Told me herself."

Scowling, the big man ducked back under the coupler and stepped out from between the boxcars. He saw the woman several cars back, taking a picture of the rear end of the train. He was about to storm over there, knock the little black box from her hand, and crush it beneath his work boot, but just then a short, brown-haired young man with a trim mustache came walking past, heading straight for the woman with the camera.

The big man cursed under his breath and gripped his crowbar tighter.

"Come on, Vinnie," Roger called.

For a moment the big man did not respond. He was still not used to that name, even though he took it from his real name—Alvin . . . Alvin McNally.

"Vinnie," the other man called again.

"Shut up," McNally grunted as he turned and walked back between the boxcars. Raising the crowbar high over his head, he swung it in an arc and brought it down violently against the coupler.

While Nora was composing a picture of the undamaged rear section of the westbound freight train, Jim Hart approached from behind and called out, "What's that you've got there, Nora?"

Spinning around, she said, "Hold it right there!"

Startled, Hart halted and looked curiously at her. It was the second she needed to click the shutter and catch him in a candid portrait.

"Perfect," she said, smiling at him.

"A camera?" he asked, coming closer. When she

nodded, he said, "But it's so small. I've never seen one like it."

"It's only been on the market for a few months. It was invented by a dry-plate manufacturer named Eastman in Rochester, New York. He calls it a Kodak." She held out the camera for him to inspect.

"What kind of name is Kodak? Does it mean something?" He took the small box and turned it over in his hands, examining it closely.

"I haven't the slightest idea. I just know that he had a good idea when he invented it."

"Where do you load the plates?" Hart asked.

"You don't. Eastman came up with a flexible gelatin film that can be rolled up. See this little lever here?" She pointed to the lever on top. "After you take a picture, you just crank that a couple of times, and the roll moves to the next section of film."

"You mean it takes more than one picture without changing film?" he asked incredulously.

She nodded. "Guess how many shots."

"I don't know. Three?"

"More."

"Five?"

She shook her head.

"Ten?"

"No. One hundred," she declared with a grin.

"You're not serious," he said in amazement.

"I didn't think it possible myself, but it is. The pictures are round—about two-and-a-half inches in diameter. All you have to do is point and click."

"Yes, but what about developing the film?" he asked.

"That's the easy part. When all one hundred shots are taken, you send the entire camera back to one of Eastman's laboratories, and they develop and print the pictures for you. Then they return the camera with a new roll of film loaded in it."

"Amazing."

"I'm surprised you haven't heard of it," Nora said.

"Who can keep up with those things? Every time you turn around, someone has invented a new kind of camera or film. I'll just wait until they all make up their minds what system we should be using, and then maybe I'll buy a camera. Until then, I'll let the professionals take the pictures."

"I'm just an amateur," Nora insisted. "But with a camera like this, everyone can take pictures like the professionals."

Suddenly Hart snapped his fingers. "That's it!" he declared.

"What?"

"Those pictures. They're exactly what I need."

"I don't understand."

"When possible, newspapers like to work from photographs when making their engravings for print. But now that I'm operating as a free lance, I don't have anyone to take pictures for me."

"With a camera like this, you could take your own," she suggested.

"Yes, but maybe for now I could make do with some of the pictures you're taking."

"These are for my brother's investigation," Nora said a bit defensively.

"I know. But with a hundred shots, perhaps you could take a few extra for me."

"I suppose so," she said hesitantly.

"Perfect. I want to do a feature about these accidents, and it would be wonderful to have pictures."

"The film has to go to a laboratory in Kansas City for developing," Nora explained, not mentioning that the laboratory was the one at the headquarters of the Faraday Security Service. "I can arrange for them to send some of the prints to whatever publication buys your story."

"You're a dear," he said, handing back the camera.

Their fingers met, and for a moment Jim Hart held his hand there, until Nora shyly turned away and withdrew her hand.

"Nora!" a voice called. "Jim!"

They turned to see Stuart Kennedy approaching.

"I was just speaking with Marshal Novak. He's over at the boxcar where the bodies were found." He indicated a car a bit closer to the engine—one of the first that did not derail during the crash.

"You'll have to get a picture!" Hart told Nora.

"I'm afraid it's too dark inside for a camera," Kennedy explained. "And Novak won't let anyone into the car."

"Isn't this out of his jurisdiction?" Hart asked.

"Yes, but he agreed to handle the preliminary investigation until a federal officer is assigned to the case."

"Surely he'll let you into the car," Hart said. "After all, you're investigating for the railroad."

"He's agreed to let me take a look around, so long as I don't disrupt any of the evidence. I just thought I'd come over first and let you know where I'd be."

"Maybe he'll let me join you and—"

"I don't think so," Kennedy replied. "He told me that he turned all the other reporters away—just gave them a statement."

"Well, if you turn up any new evidence . . ."

"You'll be the first to know," Kennedy assured him. "What will you two do in the meantime?"

"I thought I'd take some more pictures of the collision," Nora put in.

"Actually, I'd like to ride east a ways and see if I can figure out how this train switched tracks." Hart turned to Nora. "Would you like to come along?"

Nora glanced at Kennedy, who nodded and said, "I think that's a splendid idea. We can meet back here later. Maybe by then I'll have convinced the marshal to let you examine the boxcar firsthand."

With their plans decided, Nora and Hart headed over

to the carriage, while Kennedy went back to the boxcar and climbed inside.

As Kennedy's eyes adjusted to the light inside the car, he saw that Marshal Sam Novak was standing near the bodies, which lay pressed against the front wall of the car. A pair of bloody tracks along the straw-covered floor indicated that they had slid half the length of the car during the collision.

Novak glanced over at Kennedy and signaled him not to disrupt the bloody tracks as he approached. Kennedy carefully skirted the area and walked over to where the bodies lay crumpled against the wall.

"They were found just like this?" Kennedy asked.

"Yes." The marshal stroked his drooping mustache. "I'll wager the little fellow was the first to attack." He pushed the short man's body with his boot, rolling it partway onto its side. "See? He's still got the knife in his hand."

"Why do you think he attacked first?"

Novak pointed to the trails of blood. The one leading to the small man was far thinner, and there was less blood on his clothes than on the other man's. "He must've died instantly when he took the bullet. His heart stopped pumping. The other fellow died slower—messier. He'd have had time to pull his gun and fire."

Kennedy knelt beside the body of the tall man. The revolver was still held rigidly in the man's right hand. "Have you checked it?" he asked, pointing at the gun.

Novak nodded. "I spun the cylinder. One bullet was fired."

"May I?" Kennedy reached for the gun but held back until Novak motioned for him to proceed. Carefully Kennedy pried open the stiff fingers and removed the gun. He opened the chamber, then placed the gun on the floor and began examining the dead man's hands. Afterward he moved to the other body and gave it as thorough an examination.

"What do you think?" Novak asked as Kennedy stood.

"You may be right about the little man striking first—if he struck at all."

"What do you mean?"

Kennedy did not immediately respond. Instead he walked back along the bloodier of the two tracks and made a close inspection of the floor near the spot where the man fell. Finding a bloodstained bandanna, he picked it up and examined it. He then checked the area where the shorter man went down.

"Did you see this candle here?" he asked, pointing at a lump of wax that was stuck to the floor.

"I figure they used it for light," the marshal replied. "There's some melted wax on that little fellow's finger."

"Yes, I saw that." Kennedy continued to examine the floor, painstakingly running his hands across the strewn straw to make sure that he did not miss anything. Suddenly he felt a sharp prick on his left forefinger and jerked his hand back. The tip of his finger was bleeding slightly, and he squeezed it with his thumb to stop the flow. Assuming that he had struck a nail, he carefully checked the floor again and discovered that it was not a nail but a broken piece of curved glass about two inches in diameter.

"Something wrong?" the marshal asked, seeing that Kennedy was holding his left hand awkwardly.

"Just cut myself on a nailhead," Kennedy said as he rose and slipped the piece of glass into one of his jacket pockets.

"So what do you think?" Novak asked as Kennedy walked back over to him.

"I'm less convinced that the little man struck first," Kennedy said. "I'll have a better idea in a moment," he added cryptically as he stooped down and checked the soles of each man's shoes.

"What are you doing that for?" the marshal asked, genuinely curious. "They certainly didn't stomp each other to death."

"No, but somebody stomped out that candle. And it wasn't either of these men." He pointed toward the candle. "Take a look at the impression in that wax. There's a definite shoe print from a sole with a heavy tread—like a work boot. These two have smooth-soled boots, and there's no sign of wax on them."

Novak walked over to the candle and knelt beside it. Sure enough, the imprint of a work boot could be seen in the mashed lump of wax. "I think you're right," he agreed. "What do you suppose it means?"

"I think there was someone else in this car with them—someone who pulled the trigger and struck with the knife. Someone who was wearing this bandanna." He held out the bloody cloth.

"I figured it belonged to one of them," Novak explained, approaching and taking the bandanna. "Neither of these gents was wearing one."

"It could have been, but from the extent of those wounds, I doubt either man would have had the strength to untie it. See?" He showed Novak the wrinkles around two opposing corners, where the bandanna had been tied in a knot, probably around someone's neck. "Certainly that little fellow died too quickly," Kennedy added. "And the tall one was still holding his revolver."

"You've got a point there," Novak conceded. "But then again the bandanna could have been worn by one of them the day before. No, I'm not convinced that this bandanna—and that footprint in the wax—is sufficient proof that there was another killer."

"Not those things alone, but take a look at this." He beckoned the marshal closer. Raising the tall man's right hand, he continued, "This is the hand that was holding the gun. Nothing unusual in that. But look here." He raised the left hand and held them side by side. "See the stain on the middle and forefinger? Tobacco."

"So?"

"This man smoked cigarettes with his left hand. And

his left hand is noticeably more calloused, as if he used it more often. If he was wearing a holster, we'd be sure, but I'd say he was left-handed, not right."

"So you think that a third man shot the little man, then put the gun in this man's hand to make it look like he pulled the trigger?"

"Precisely. And the killer did the same thing with the knife."

"But there's no sign of a struggle," Novak pointed out.

"Most likely these men were asleep—or unconscious —at the time."

Novak scratched his head in wonderment. "I never would've guessed that a man who wears a suit and sits in an office all day would be so good at examining evidence."

"I'm an insurance investigator, remember?"

"Yes, but since when has insurance become such a dangerous business?"

"You'd be surprised," Kennedy replied with a grin.

"One other thing," Novak said as Kennedy started toward the boxcar door. "Any idea if these murders were connected to the train crash?"

"It would be a mighty big coincidence if they weren't," Kennedy declared. He stepped into the open doorway, then looked back at the marshal. "Is there any way we can keep my theory a secret—at least for the time being?"

"Why?"

"For the moment it's the only lead we have that isn't public knowledge. It may give us an edge against whoever is responsible for these crashes."

"That sounds like a good idea," the marshal replied. "I'll see to it."

"Thank you."

"One thing, though," Novak added.

"Yes?"

"If you figure out who caused all of this, don't try to take him on alone. You insurance boys may be good at examining a dead man with a gun in the wrong hand, but it's another thing going up against a live one who knows which finger pulls the trigger."

"Don't worry. I'm not looking to be a hero," Kennedy assured him.

"Good. Because you know the one thing that most men who try to be heros have in common? . . . They get killed."

"Whoa! Hold up there!" Jim Hart called to the horses as he pulled back on the reins.

"What is it?" Nora asked, looking across the grassy plain to the raised gravel roadbed. They had been riding on the carriage road for some time and were at a point where the tracks were about one hundred yards away.

"Look at that," Hart said, pointing back along the road a short distance to the spot they had just passed. In the soft dirt at the shoulder were a couple of pairs of carriage tracks that curved away from the road and headed toward the train tracks.

Hart slapped the reins gently and turned the horses in a circle, bringing the phaeton back to where the tracks led across the field. He glanced at Nora, who nodded for him to proceed. Clucking at the animals, he turned the carriage off the road and followed the tracks toward the railroad.

Hart halted the phaeton about halfway to the tracks. "They stop here, then turn and go back to the road," he said. "It almost seems as if someone sat here in some kind of a buggy watching the tracks."

"And look," Nora said, pointing excitedly to the hoofprints in the area. "Some are from the horse that pulled the buggy. But those over there are from a single horse. See the way they approach and then return to the tracks?"

"Let's check it out." Hart set the brake and jumped from the phaeton. He helped Nora down, and together they followed the hoofprints over to the raised roadbed.

It took them a little while to figure out what had happened, but then the evidence was unmistakable. Enough gravel had been overturned to show that a large group of people had been working in the area—a group that included horses and at least one wagon. What the people had been up to was plain enough to see when Jim Hart discovered the place where each of the tracks recently had been disconnected and then rejoined. After he and Nora had closely examined the gravel between the two sets of tracks, they were able to identify the depressions where temporary ties had been laid and the two sets of rails had been connected together.

"This is where it happened," Hart stated with conviction as Nora went around taking pictures of the rails and the roadbed. "God only knows why they did it—but this is the place."

Lowering her camera, Nora came over and stood beside Hart. "The crew must have been knocked out first," she theorized. "Afterward, the westbound train was moved to the other track at this makeshift shunt. Then the tracks were returned to their normal condition and the train went on its way. The crew was probably still on board, since they were found later at the river, wandering around in a daze."

"Someone else must have been driving," Hart added. "At the river he unloaded the crew, set the throttle, and jumped clear. The same thing would have happened to the eastbound train, but without its having to switch tracks."

Nora looked over at Hart. "It looks like you've got the lead for your story—one that nobody else will have."

Hart nodded slowly. "I only wish it didn't come at the cost of so much destruction, though I suppose that without a little destruction now and then, there'd be no need for reporters."

"Well, as long as the world needs reporters, you can be proud that you're one of the best." She smiled at Hart, then tugged at his sleeve. "Come on. Let's get back and tell Stuart."

They hurried down the raised roadbed and back to the phaeton. A moment later Hart whipped the horses to a gallop, and they went careening back along the carriage road toward the place where the pair of freight trains had met their fate head-on.

Chapter 6

THE MORNING AFTER RETURNING FROM THE SITE OF THE SEC-
ond train collision, Jim Hart joined Nora Sutherland
and Stuart Kennedy at breakfast in the hotel dining
room. As they drank coffee and waited for their meals to
be served, Nora eyed the young reporter, who seemed
unable to stop grinning. "You seem in a particularly
chipper mood today," she said.

"And why shouldn't he?" Kennedy put in. "His story
will hit the stands today, and the rest of the newsboys
around here will be left with egg on their faces." Hart's
grin broadened. "I have to admit it feels good being the
one to break the news about how the train ended up on
the wrong track."

"You also proved conclusively that there was foul play
involved," Kennedy added. "And an elaborate scheme,
at that."

"But since you sold your story to newspapers back
east, won't it take a few days for those papers to make it
back out here?" Nora asked.

"That's the beauty of it." Hart put down his coffee and

leaned forward, his voice lowering to a hush. "As a free lance, I can sell my story anywhere—and that's precisely what I did. Not only are half a dozen papers from Chicago to New York running it, but early this morning I sold the local rights to the *Denver Post,* the chief rival of my former employer. They're running it this morning with the byline, *Jim Hart, Special Correspondent.*"

"You should be very proud," Nora told him.

"It wouldn't have happened without the two of you," Hart insisted. "Thanks for all your assistance."

Kennedy waved off the remark. "Nonsense, Jim. You were the one who saw those buggy tracks and discovered where the break in the rails was made. You didn't need us for that." He lowered his eyes and took another sip of coffee, covering the pang of guilt that he felt for not yet having filled in the reporter on the evidence he had turned up in the boxcar.

"Maybe so," Hart replied, "but then again, maybe not. I've learned that if you change one element of an event, the entire outcome may turn out differently."

"Well, whatever the contributing factors, you've a right to be proud."

Hart was smirking with delight. "I know it's terrible of me, but I wish I could see the faces at *The Rocky Mountain News* when they get a look at the front page of the *Post.*"

"There's nothing wrong with gloating a little, especially after the way they treated your last story," Nora said.

"I don't know. Maybe I've been too hard on them. After all, it was really only one person who kept my story from running."

"Whatever became of that fellow, anyway?" Kennedy asked.

"Timothy Blaine? I heard that he was given three days in jail for disturbing the peace. He'll be released tomorrow."

"I just hope he's learned his lesson," Nora remarked.

"After the way you handled him," Hart marveled, "I'd

say he'd have a hard time forgetting." He grinned at Nora, and she blushed slightly.

"There you are!" a voice called from across the dining room, and they looked over to see a red-haired man approaching from the lobby. It was the same reporter who had spoken to Jim Hart when they first arrived at the crash site the previous afternoon. "Hiding out at your hotel when everybody is looking for you? Aren't you ashamed?" The man gave a mock frown.

"Uh, Mike, I don't think I properly introduced you to my friends," Hart said a bit disconcertedly. "This is Stuart Kennedy and his sister, Nora Sutherland. And this is Mike Spayne. He's with the *Denver Post*."

"Not for long, if you keep getting the beat on me like this." He produced a folded newspaper from under his arm. Opening it, he pointed to Jim Hart's byline on the lead article. "Bumped me right off my own front page. Is that a way to treat a friend? And after I gave you all that information yesterday."

"I . . . I'm sorry."

Spayne grinned and slapped Hart on the back. "I'm just pulling your leg. It wasn't your fault you got lucky, and I don't hold it against you. Just don't make it a habit!"

"I'll try not to."

"Do you mind . . . ?" Spayne asked, indicating the empty chair at the table.

"Of course not. Please . . . sit down."

"Perhaps you'd like to order some breakfast," Nora offered.

"Thank you, ma'am, but I've already eaten." He narrowed one eye at Hart. "Had myself a couple of drinks, too, thanks to you."

"I'm really sorry."

Spayne laughed aloud. "Forget it, friend. It was worth it to see the faces on the boys from *The Rocky Mountain News* this morning. They're really fuming over this one, you know."

Hart allowed himself a grin. "I would like to have been there."

"You'll get your chance," Spayne promised. "Everyone's looking for you."

"Me?"

"Of course. You've become part of the news. They say the *Rocky Mountain* editor turned blue when he had to assign one of his boys to interview you for a story about yesterday's discovery."

"It really wasn't anything special," Hart began. "I just—"

"Not special? Hell, it's the talk of the town!" He abruptly turned to Nora and added, "Excuse my language, ma'am, but we reporters are an excitable breed."

"So I'm learning," she said with a smile.

"Well, what about it?" Spayne asked, turning back to Hart. "Are you going to give me that interview first, or do I have to wait in line with everyone else?"

"Of course I will."

Just then the waitress appeared with their food.

"Eat hearty," Spayne said as the waitress served Hart his order of eggs and potatoes. "I'll wait in the lobby until you're finished." He rose and smiled at Kennedy and Nora. "I'm sorry for intruding. It's been a pleasure to meet you both." He spun on his heels and walked away.

"How does it feel?" Nora asked Hart as soon as the man was gone from the dining room.

"What do you mean?"

"Being a celebrity."

Hart stared down at his food and frowned slightly. "It gives me indigestion."

"You'll have to get used to it," Kennedy said. He nodded toward the open doorway to the lobby. "I think another of your admirers is about to present himself."

Hart turned and caught sight of a thin, brown-haired man in a red-checkered shirt who was looking toward them. But then the man abruptly turned and strode away across the lobby. Hart stared after him for a moment, and then he turned back in the chair and shook his head. "I don't recognize him. He must have wanted someone else."

"Well, you'd better eat up," Nora put in, pointing her knife at Hart's plate. "You'll need your strength to face those admiring hordes."

Hart gingerly picked up his fork and stabbed at a piece of potato. He started to raise it to his lips, then lowered the fork. "I . . . I seem to have lost my appetite."

Outside the Orient Hotel, the man in the checkered shirt hurried down the street and ducked into an alley beside the hotel. A far bigger man was waiting there, and he gave an impatient scowl as the thin, sharp-featured man approached.

"What'd you see, Benny?" the big man asked, lifting his hat off his greasy black hair and rubbing his brow. It was Alvin McNally, and he was speaking to his right-hand man, Benny Armatrading.

"He's in there, all right—in the dining room," Armatrading told him. "How did you know?"

"I asked around after he left the site of the wreck yesterday and found out he's a reporter with *The Rocky Mountain News*. When we got back to the rail yard last night, I visited the paper and learned he doesn't work there anymore but lives at the Orient."

"What are you going to do?" Armatrading asked.

"I don't care about him. It's his photographer friend I want. Was she with him?"

"He was sitting with a man and a woman."

"What does she look like?"

"Brown hair, in her twenties or so, real pretty . . ."

"And the man?"

"Pretty tall, solid looking, light-brown hair, clean shaven . . ."

"That's the one—some kind of insurance investigator

for the railroad. All three rode back to Denver together in a carriage."

"So what's the plan?" Armatrading asked.

"I want that camera," McNally declared. "You're gonna have to go back in there and find out what room—"

"I think they saw me."

"What?"

"They all looked over at me, so I beat it out of there real quick."

"You idiot!" McNally raised a fist as if to strike the smaller man, then held back.

"I'll go back if you want, but—"

"No, forget it." He lowered his fist and leaned back against the brick wall of the hotel. "She saw me out at the crash site, so I can't go in there, either. I'll have to get one of the other boys to check the register. Then we'll keep watch on the place. When she goes out somewhere, I'll break into her room and destroy that camera."

"And if it isn't there?"

"Then we'll just have to make her tell us where it's gone." McNally stood away from the wall. "C'mon, Benny. We've got work to do."

McNally led the way to the alley entrance, glancing out a moment to make sure that no one was looking. Then he stepped out from the alley and briskly led the way down the street to where their horses were tied.

Later that morning, Stuart Kennedy left the Orient Hotel and hailed a gurney cab to take him to Harold Trimm's pharmacy on Larimer Street. Pulling up in front of the establishment, he climbed down and asked the cabbie to wait for him. He entered the store to find Trimm busy with a mother and daughter who were purchasing a wide array of items. From their banter, Kennedy surmised that the younger woman was betrothed and soon would be setting up her own home.

Harold Trimm glanced up at Kennedy and nodded with recognition, signaling that he would be free momentarily. Then he went back to describing in glowing terms the virtues of one particular bath lotion and its advantages over regular soap.

As Kennedy waited, he circled the store and examined the products, which ranged from patent medicines such as cough syrups and headache powders to toothpastes and shaving soaps. One glass case held an assortment of straight razors and several brands of the double-sided safety razors that recently were becoming the vogue.

A few minutes later, the women had made their purchases and departed.

"I was expecting to see you," Trimm said, his tone less than enthusiastic. "I'm afraid I've failed."

"What do you mean?" Kennedy asked, coming over to the counter.

"I've put together a list of a number of chemicals that under varying circumstances meet the criteria you set forth. And with all the possible compounds that can be formed from those chemicals, the list really does go on and on. If I only had more to go on. . . ."

"Perhaps this will help," Kennedy declared, reaching into his jacket pocket. He withdrew a folded handkerchief, which he placed on the counter and carefully unfolded to reveal a two-inch-diameter fragment of glass. "I found it at the site of yesterday's crash."

Trimm bent over and eyed the clear, curved piece of glass. He started to touch it, then pulled back his hand, as if afraid he might contaminate a piece of evidence. "Such a tragedy," he remarked, shaking his head. He slipped his hand under the handkerchief and lifted the broken piece of glass in front of his eyes. "And you think this glass is somehow connected?"

"It could be part of a bottle that held the chemical that knocked out those crewmen," Kennedy suggested. "Such a container could have been tossed at their feet without anyone seeing who did it."

"Yes, I see." Trimm held the glass to his nose and sniffed. "I don't smell anything, but if it's as you say, it probably evaporated. However, there 'should still be traces of the compound on this glass."

"Can you find out what it is?"

"If there's something on this glass, I'll figure it out. I'll have to break the glass into smaller pieces, though, and test each one for a different chemical. Is that all right?"

"Of course. How long do you think it will take?"

Trimm looked around the pharmacy and then turned to Kennedy and smiled. "Business has been terribly slow this week. And it's lunchtime, so I suppose there's no harm in closing for a few hours. Perhaps if you come back around six o'clock, I'll have a better idea."

"Thank you." Kennedy turned to leave.

"One other thing," Trimm called after him.

"I know," Kennedy said, opening the front door and looking back at him. "Turn the sign and lock the door."

Trimm smiled and nodded.

As Kennedy reversed the sign and turned the lock, Harold Trimm was already disappearing through the back door into his private laboratory. Kennedy grinned and shook his head, then pulled the door shut and walked back to the waiting cab.

"The telegraph office," he called to the driver as he climbed aboard.

With a tip of his hat, the driver snatched up the reins, lightly flicked the whip above the horse's head, and started the cab at a brisk walk down Larimer Street.

Just down the street from Harold Trimm's pharmacy, Alvin McNally dismounted and tied the reins of his horse to a hitch rail.

"Aren't we gonna keep following him?" Benny Armatrading asked, looking down at his boss from the saddle of his bay gelding.

McNally stared after the departing gurney cab, then looked up at Armatrading. "You follow him and see what else he's up to. I want to find out what he told that druggist."

"What'll I do then?" Armatrading asked with an anxious edge to his voice.

"Just see where he goes. I'll meet you back at the saloon near the hotel, where the other boys are waiting. Now get going before you lose him."

Armatrading pulled back on the reins and turned his gelding out into the street. Kicking the animal's sides, he followed after the horse-drawn cab.

McNally, patting his horse's muzzle, stepped up onto the sidewalk and approached the pharmacy. Seeing the sign marked *Closed,* he leaned near the glass and peered inside. The store appeared to be empty, but at the back he could see an open door that apparently led to another room.

Testing the doorknob, McNally discovered it locked. He glanced up and down the street to make sure that no one was watching, then reached under his coat and drew out a heavy, wide-bladed bowie knife. Standing close to the door, he pressed the edge of the blade between the door and the jamb and ran it up and down until he found the locking bolt. After he had forced the blade in a bit farther, he levered the knife handle to the right, spreading apart the door and the jamb. With a loud pop, the bolt slipped from the holder on the jamb, and the door swung open.

Stepping into the shop, McNally unlocked the bolt so that he could close the door again, and then he relocked it and put away his knife. Quietly, he made his way through the shop toward the open rear door. As he approached, he could hear someone working and smelled the pungent odor of chemicals.

Standing in the doorway, McNally saw Harold Trimm on the far side of the laboratory, pouring some sort of liquid into a flask at the worktable on the right side of the alley door. He watched as the druggist picked up a small fragment of glass in a long pair of tweezers and lowered it into the flask, then withdrew it. The druggist held the glass to the light of the window and shook his head.

"What's that you've got there?" McNally called in an unusually pleasant voice.

Startled, Trimm dropped the tweezers and spun around. "Who . . . who are you?" he asked.

"The name's Johnson . . . Al Johnson," McNally lied. "May I come in?"

"But how did you get in here?"

"What do you mean?" McNally asked innocently. "The sign said closed, but the door was unlocked."

"He must have forgotten," Trimm muttered to himself, then said to the visitor, "If you require something from the store—"

"No, I'm not a customer." McNally smiled pleasantly as he stepped into the laboratory and approached the right-hand worktable. "I work for the railroad. I'm looking for one of our insurance investigators—"

"Oh, you mean Mr. Kennedy."

"That's right."

"You just missed him," Trimm said. "He left here not five minutes ago."

"Oh, that's too bad. Did he say where he was going?"

"No. Back to his hotel, I suppose. I'll be seeing him when he returns later, so I can give him a message if you—"

"He's coming back?"

"This evening—to get the test results."

"Oh, yes." McNally nodded, as if just recalling some forgotten incident. "Mr. Kennedy mentioned that you were carrying out some tests for him." He glanced beyond the druggist to the objects on the worktable. "Have you had any luck so far?"

"Not yet, but I'm sure I'll pin it down soon."

"May I take a look?" McNally asked, motioning toward the table.

Trimm seemed uncomfortable, but he made no effort to stop the big man from approaching.

McNally came up to the table and glanced briefly at the various flasks and bottles of chemicals. His attention was immediately drawn to a curved fragment of glass, half of which was intact, with the other half in small pieces that lay scattered around the larger one.

"From the train, isn't it?"

"Uh, yes," Trimm replied.

McNally picked up the large piece and held it to the light. "And you're trying to determine what this glass may have been holding." When Trimm did not reply, McNally turned toward him and gave a smug grin. "Have you tried diethyl ether?"

Trimm looked at him curiously. "I . . . I was just going to test for that."

"I think you'll discover that your test proves positive."

"But it could also be—"

"It's diethyl ether," McNally stated flatly.

"How do you know?" Trimm asked. "The only way—" He swallowed the words as he realized how this big, ominous-looking stranger knew so certainly what the test results would produce. "My God!" he gasped as he turned to run from the laboratory.

McNally saw the move coming and struck like a snake, leaping at his prey and slamming into him full force before Trimm had gotten halfway across the room.

The druggist went down with a groan as the air rushed out of him. Gasping for breath, he flopped around on his belly as a pair of viselike hands grabbed hold of his shoulders and tried to roll him onto his back. His arms flailed about as he struggled to free himself from the far bigger man, who straddled his back now and snaked an arm around his neck, yanking backward and cutting off his windpipe.

Trimm summoned what remained of his strength and gave one mighty heave, throwing his hips upward off the floor. Caught by surprise, McNally went sprawling forward off Trimm's back, his arm releasing its grip. Trimm was up in an instant, gagging and choking as he looked around for a means of escape. McNally had landed in front of the doorway to the store, so Trimm turned and ran toward the door that led to the back alley. He was just grabbing at the knob when he felt steely fingers dig into his shoulders and spin him around.

Trimm caught a glimpse of McNally's grinning face, and then a wild haymaker seemed to come out of nowhere, smashing into his jaw. He felt himself being propelled away from the door, his body careening into the left-hand worktable. Bottles and flasks went flying everywhere, smashing against the wall and floor. Trying not to lose consciousness, Trimm grabbed at one of the bottles and managed to grasp it around the neck. As the big man closed in, he swung it wildly but missed the man's head by inches.

Cursing, McNally swatted the bottle out of the smaller man's hand as if it were a pesky fly, then grasped Trimm's coat lapels and threw him down against the table, which was covered in a thin, gaseous haze from the spilled and broken bottles of chemicals. There was a dull thud as his skull struck the hard surface, and then his eyes rolled back in his head.

Holding Trimm in place, McNally grabbed him by the hair and repeatedly slammed his head against the table. When he finally let the man's lifeless body slide to the floor, the tabletop was covered with a swirling pool of chemicals and blood, resembling a red, mist-shrouded lake.

McNally stood away from the table and admired his handiwork; he did not have to check the man's pulse to know that he was dead.

Crossing to the right-hand worktable, he gathered up the pieces of glass, holding them gingerly in the palm of his hand. He started into the store, then thought better of it and headed over to the rear exit. Turning the knob, he pulled open the door and slipped outside.

McNally stared up and down the alley to make sure it was empty. Pulling the door shut behind him, he made his way toward the street but stopped after a few feet and dropped the glass to the ground. Raising his boot, he stomped on it several times until it was pulverized, then kicked dirt over it until all traces were gone. He proceeded down the alley and returned to where his horse was tied.

As the big man rode back along Larimer Street toward the Orient Hotel, he plotted the tasks that remained to be completed before he could return to the gang's hideout. He had not yet had an opportunity to break into that woman's room and destroy the picture she had taken of him. And there was still that insurance man named Kennedy to deal with.

The druggist had said that Kennedy would be returning to the pharmacy later that evening. McNally would see to it that he never got there alive . . . and that any knowledge of those bottles of diethyl ether died along with him.

Chapter 7

ALVIN MCNALLY AND BENNY ARMATRADING WERE STANDING with another gang member on the front porch of a saloon just down the street from the Orient Hotel. "What's taking him so long?" McNally said in annoyance as he stared toward the hotel.

"Willie'll be along as soon as either of them goes anywhere," Armatrading assured him.

"They've been up in their rooms a long time." He glowered at Armatrading. "Are you sure that Kennedy fellow didn't go anywhere but the telegraph office?"

"That's it—I swear. He stopped in there for a while, then went straight back to the hotel."

McNally looked up at the sky to gauge the time. "Well, he'll be leaving soon enough to go back to the pharmacy."

"That's when we take him," the third man said.

"Yes—you, Benny, and Willie. And I don't want any mistakes." He lowered his voice. "He's got to be killed."

"Don't worry," the third man said. "We'll take care of it—just the way we planned."

"See that you do."

"Are you sure you don't want one of us to stay here and help you?" Armatrading asked.

McNally shook his head. "It'll go smoother alone. I'll just slip into her room, and if she's there—" He drew a finger across his throat. "If not, I'll just take care of the camera and be gone."

"Here comes Willie," the third man announced, nodding down the street.

McNally and Armatrading looked to see a tall, lanky cowboy sauntering along the street from the direction of the Orient Hotel. He came straight over to the saloon and stood in the street, leaning against the porch rail.

"The man and his sister just came down to the lobby. He's dressed to go out. I think she's staying to have dinner with that reporter fellow—at least that's what she told her brother."

"Did they see you?" McNally asked.

"They didn't pay me no attention. I was playing cards with one of the old-timers."

"Good. You got the lady's room number?"

"Here." He handed McNally a slip of paper on which he had written the number three hundred seventeen. "It's on the third floor. His room's next door in three nineteen."

"There he is," Armatrading said, motioning toward the hotel. Stuart Kennedy had just come out and was speaking with the doorman. A moment later, the doorman walked down to the curb and stood looking up and down for a passing cab to hail.

"You know what you're to do, Chris?" McNally asked the third man.

"Don't worry. I'll get him over to the rail yard."

"Good. Benny and Willie will be waiting where we planned. Just see that you get him there."

Chris nodded and started off the porch to where the horses were tied.

"Don't worry about nothin', boss," the one named Willie said. He followed Chris over to the horses.

As Armatrading started after them, McNally called, "When you finish the job, get back to the hideout. I'll meet you there." Pointing toward a gurney cab that was just pulling away from the hotel, he added, "Get going, now."

The three men mounted up and pulled back from the hitch rail. Armatrading and Willie turned their horses in a circle and started away from the hotel, in the direction of the rail yard. Chris, meanwhile, spurred his horse to a trot and took off after the cab.

A few blocks from the Orient Hotel, Stuart Kennedy jerked to attention as the gurney cab lurched to the side and came to an abrupt halt.

"What's going on?" the cabbie shouted at a young man on horseback who had overtaken the vehicle and forced it to the side of the road.

Kennedy instinctively reached under his coat, ready to draw his Smith & Wesson if necessary as he waited to hear what the young rider had to say.

"Sorry," the rider apologized with a smile as he raised his hand in greeting. "I have to speak with your passenger." He kneed his horse closer to the cab. "Are you Mr. Kennedy?" he asked in an innocent tone, holding his hands in plain view as if pointedly not wishing to alarm anyone.

"Why do you want to know?" Kennedy asked, leaning forward in the seat.

"I got a message for him. When I arrived at the Orient, the doorman said he'd just gone 'round the corner in a cab, and this is the only one in sight."

"What's the message?" Kennedy asked without admitting who he was.

"It's from Marshal Novak. He wants to see this Mr. Kennedy over at the rail yard right away. Something about some new evidence on those boxcars they brought in from that crash yesterday."

Kennedy eyed the man closely, gauging the sincerity of his smile. "Are you certain he wants to see me now?"

"If your name's Kennedy he does."

"It is," Kennedy stated. Turning to the driver, he said, "Follow this man to the rail yard, please."

With a shrug, the cabbie took up the reins and started the vehicle down the street again, turning at the next corner toward the rail yard. The young man on the horse rode alongside, every now and then glancing over at Kennedy and smiling.

As they neared the rail yard ten minutes later, the young horseman directed the cabbie down a back street. "The marshal's over there," he said, pointing into the distance.

It was growing dark as the sun dipped below the horizon, but even in the gray light of dusk Kennedy could see that the man was indicating a row of boxcars in a deserted section of the yard.

At the young man's direction, the cabbie pulled up at a gate, which was too narrow to allow passage by the cab. Kennedy climbed out, directing the cabbie to wait there for him to return. Then he followed on foot as the horseman rode through the gate and led the way to the boxcars.

Kennedy found himself growing increasingly suspicious as he walked through the shadows. He slipped his hand under his coat and kept it on the butt of his Smith & Wesson as they circled some of the stray cars in the yard and approached the row of boxcars the man had indicated.

Kennedy saw the twin muzzle flashes before he heard the reports or felt the wind of a bullet whining past his cheek. He leaped to the ground and went into a roll, drawing his gun and firing at the place one of the flashes had been, then five feet or so to the right, where he had seen the second flash. He thought he heard a wounded cry, and then a single shot rang out, but the bullet whizzed overhead, again missing him by mere inches.

Kennedy's roll took him almost directly under the legs of the young man's horse, causing the animal to shy back and rear up. This effectively kept the man busy, so that his revolver had not yet been brought into play. But as he calmed and steadied the animal, he clawed at his gun and aimed at the spot where Kennedy had landed.

Kennedy was no longer there, for after firing the second shot he had continued to roll to the side, coming up on the other side of the horse. As the rider searched for him, he knew that he could plug him in the back and finish him off. But this man might be the only link to the person who destroyed those trains and orchestrated this ambush.

Holstering his revolver, Kennedy lunged forward, grabbed the rider from behind, and dragged him down off the horse, causing the man's gun to fire harmlessly into the air as he fell. The man landed on his back with a thud, and Kennedy stomped on his wrist. When the young man released the gun, Kennedy kicked it into the shadows.

As the frightened horse reared up and galloped away into the darkness, Kennedy reached down and yanked the man to his feet. When the man swung wildly to defend himself, Kennedy unleashed a vicious right to the jaw, stunning him. He followed with an uppercut deep into the man's belly, doubling him over and dropping him to his knees. The fight was finished that quickly, with the young man on his hands and knees, choking and gasping for breath.

Kennedy drew his gun and listened. He heard someone running away along the tracks, and he raised his gun and shouted, "Halt!" When the footsteps continued, he aimed in that direction and pulled the trigger. He thought he heard the footsteps receding into the distance, and then all was silent, save for the gasping of the man on the ground.

Keeping his revolver trained on his opponent, Kennedy walked over and retrieved the gun he had kicked away. "Come on," he said as he returned to the man and yanked him to his feet. "Walk!" He prodded him in the back with the barrel of his gun.

The sky was still light enough for Kennedy to make out their surroundings as he pushed his prisoner over toward where the ambushers had been hiding. It did not take long to find the spot—or the body of a man struck in the chest by one of Kennedy's bullets.

"He . . . he's dead," the young man stammered as he looked down at the body.

"A friend of yours?" Kennedy asked, but the prisoner fell silent.

Kennedy checked the area but saw no sign of the other gunman, who had apparently escaped unscathed.

"Let's get going," he said, poking the young man with his gun barrel. "You've scared off the horse and probably my cabbie, so it looks like we'll be walking to the marshal's."

The walk proved to be far shorter than Kennedy had expected, for though he was correct in assuming that the gurney cab would be gone, the cabbie had driven directly to the marshal's office to report the shooting. Soon the marshal and one of his deputies arrived on horseback, led to the scene by the cabbie.

Before heading to the jail, Kennedy took the two lawmen to the body of the dead ambusher. He was a stranger to both of them, but Novak promised to check the wanted posters to see if they could identify him.

After slinging the body over the marshal's horse, the deputy mounted his own horse and led it off to the undertaker's. Then Novak and Kennedy climbed into the cab, with the prisoner seated between them, and headed off to the jail. As they rode, the marshal interrogated the prisoner, but the young man was steadfast in refusing to divulge any information.

The building that housed the marshal's office and jail at first seemed to Kennedy to be far too small to serve the needs of a city as large as Denver. Novak explained that it was the original marshal's office, constructed at a time when Denver was a fraction of its present size. At the front was the main office area, with desks for a couple of deputies, one of whom was currently on duty. A door to one side led to the marshal's private office. Just behind the front room was a cellblock with four cells, which were used to house short-term prisoners such as Timothy Blaine, who currently was the only person incarcerated there.

As they entered the jail and brought the young prisoner to the cell across from Blaine's, the marshal told Kennedy that the rapid growth of the city had forced them to build a larger jailhouse, where prisoners sentenced to longer terms were housed. It was down the street and overseen by a deputy, who was assisted by several guards. Furthermore, there were a couple of other offices in different sections of the city, each under the charge of a pair of deputies, with all the offices linked by a crude telephone system.

Once the prisoner was locked up in back, Kennedy and Novak met alone in the marshal's office. Kennedy began by recounting the events of the evening, while Novak took notes on a large legal pad. As Kennedy was finishing, Novak looked up from the pad, cocked his head slightly, and asked, "Now, why do you think those three fellows would be interested in an insurance investigator like you?"

Kennedy weighed what he might say, finally resolving that the time had come for candor. "I'm afraid I haven't been entirely truthful with you." He reached into his pocket and produced a thin wallet, which he flipped open and placed on the desk in front of the marshal. Showing through a window was Kennedy's identification card from the Faraday Security Service.

"I thought as much," Novak said, examining the card and then pushing the wallet back toward Kennedy.

"I'm sorry. Actually, when we met out at the crash site, I was not officially on the case yet. I got involved because I happened to be on hand following the first crash. It wasn't until earlier today, when I telegraphed our headquarters in Kansas City, that I was informed that the Union Pacific has hired us to investigate these incidents. Only at that point was I empowered to take the local law authorities into my confidence."

"I understand," Novak said, waving off Kennedy's concerns. "From the way you handled that evidence in the boxcar, I guessed you were more than an insurance man, but I figured you'd fill me in when you were ready." He paused and looked down at his notes. "You said you wired Faraday headquarters today?" he asked. "Think there might be a connection with this ambush?"

"Not really. I worked the telegraph key myself and was patched in directly to the office. I doubt the message was compromised."

"There's always the chance these boys are mad at you for some other case you've been involved in—something unrelated to the train collisions."

"I don't think so. If that were true, why would they set up the ambush at the rail yard? No, I'm convinced there's a connection to this case."

"I think you're right," the marshal agreed. "But something must've set them off. Maybe they've been following you for a time. Where did you say you were going in that cab tonight?" He again scanned his notes.

"Over to Harold Trimm's pharmacy on Larimer Street. I have him investigating some of the evidence I've come up with." Suddenly Kennedy snapped his fingers. "That must be it!" he exclaimed. "I was there earlier today, just before I went to the telegraph office. Maybe one of them followed me and . . ." His jaw suddenly dropped. "Oh, no!"

"What is it?"

"That druggist . . . if he told them anything . . ."

"We'd better get over there," Novak declared, pushing back his chair and standing. Hurrying out into the main room, he turned to the lone deputy on duty. "Carlisle, we're going to Harold Trimm's pharmacy on Larimer Street. Bertram has my horse over at the undertaker's, so we'll use yours and the spare one out back." Without waiting for a reply, he spun around and rushed from the office, with Kennedy close behind.

A few minutes later, the horses were saddled, and the two men were riding at a gallop toward Larimer Street, about two miles away. Pulling to a halt in front of the pharmacy, they leaped from their horses and tied them to the hitch rail. Kennedy saw at once that the *Closed* sign was still up and that no lanterns had been lit inside. He tried the doorknob, but it was locked.

Drawing his Smith & Wesson, Kennedy was about to smash the door glass with the revolver butt when Novak grabbed his arm and said, "Around back."

The two men raced down the street to a narrow alley that led behind the buildings. A minute later they were standing outside Trimm's private laboratory, which was just as dark as the store.

The marshal tried the rear door and found it unlocked. With his gun raised and cocked, he pushed the door open and entered at a crouch, moving the gun from side to side. Kennedy followed close behind, the two men fanning out on either side of the door after they were both inside.

"Seems empty," Novak whispered, though it was difficult to tell in the darkness. "I'll light a lantern." He pulled a match from his shirt pocket and struck it against one of the tables. As he held it aloft, they simultaneously saw the body of a man lying crumpled on the floor.

"Damn!" Novak muttered as Kennedy stooped beside the body and confirmed that it was Harold Trimm.

The match burned low, and Novak shook it out and lit another. Looking around, he found a lantern on the right-hand worktable, which had not been disrupted during the attack. A moment later he had it lit and had adjusted the wick.

"He took quite a beating," Novak said as he held the lantern over the body. "What happened to his face?"

Grasping the dead man's hair, Kennedy tilted the head toward the light. The entire right side of the face was hideously burned, with sections of white bone showing beneath what remained of the skin.

Standing, Kennedy examined the table just above the body. Numerous bottles had been knocked over and broken, their contents having mixed together to form the caustic acid that had run off the table and onto the dead man's face, burning half of it away.

Kennedy again knelt beside the body, lifting the head and checking underneath, all the while taking care not to touch any spot that might still retain some of the acid. "He was beaten to death," Kennedy finally pronounced, lowering the head. "His skull is crushed. The burn happened after he was lying here dead."

Kennedy stood away from the body. He found a second lantern on the rolltop desk and lit it, then began to search the room for any sign of the piece of glass that he had given the druggist to analyze. Novak, meanwhile, checked the dead man's pockets in the hope of turning up some piece of evidence that might point to his killer.

"Exactly what was your business with Trimm?" the marshal asked as they continued their investigation.

"He was trying to figure out what chemical might have been used to knock out the train crews."

"Then you believe their story about smelling a mysterious gas?"

"After what's happened here, don't you?"

"You have a point," Novak admitted. "Did Trimm ever figure it out?"

"I don't know. I was on my way over here tonight to find out."

"It looks like we may never know."

Across the room, Kennedy was searching the top of the worktable that had not been disrupted during the attack. Seeing something glitter in the light, he held the lantern closer and carefully examined the tabletop. Then he saw it: a small fragment of glass, little more than a quarter inch square. From its thinness and the way it had a slight curve, Kennedy was convinced that it was from the larger piece he had given Harold Trimm to examine. Kennedy figured that whoever killed Trimm had taken the rest of the glass but had overlooked this one fragment.

There was a clean piece of cloth on the table, and Kennedy wrapped it around the glass and slipped the packet into his coat pocket. He decided against showing it to Novak. If he were to do so, he might have to turn it over to the marshal. And since he could not be completely certain that this fragment was from the piece he had given Harold Trimm, he felt justified in waiting until the Faraday lab had had a chance to analyze it.

Just then Marshal Novak stood away from the body and said, "There's nothing much to go on here. I'll have the body taken away and carry out a more thorough examination in the morning."

The marshal was interrupted by the sound of someone banging furiously on the front door of the pharmacy. With lanterns in hand, the two men hurried into the main room and saw a figure silhouetted against the door. The figure appeared to be stooped over with his hands on his knees, as if he was panting.

"It's Deputy Carlisle," Novak declared as they approached the door. The marshal quickly unlocked it and pulled it open. "What happened?" he asked as the deputy stumbled into the room.

"I . . . I ran all the way," he said, gasping for air. "You . . . t-took the horses."

"What do you want?"

"Me?" Carlisle said in surprise, slowly catching his breath. "You're the one who . . . who sent for me."

"What are you talking about?" Novak asked impatiently.

The young deputy looked back and forth between his boss and Kennedy. "Didn't you send for me?"

"I don't know what you're talking about."

"But someone came in and—"

"Who?"

"I don't know . . . some big guy with dark hair. He came running in and said you needed me right away. I dropped everything and came running." Seeing the marshal's confused expression, he hesitantly asked, "Didn't you send for me?"

"Of course not. It must have been a prank."

"Wait a minute!" Kennedy grasped the marshal's arm, then turned to the deputy. "Was there another deputy on duty when you left?"

"No. Bertram hadn't come back yet."

"Maybe that fellow who got away from me tonight decided to return and spring his partner," Kennedy suggested. "And he didn't want any deputies around when he did."

"You fool!" Novak blared. "You left those prisoners unguarded?"

"B-but . . . they're locked up," Carlisle pointed out. "And I took the keys." He produced a ring of keys from his pocket and held it aloft.

Kennedy glanced ominously toward the laboratory door. "From what we've seen of the men who killed Harold Trimm, I'd say he might not need any keys to make sure that his partner doesn't talk."

"C'mon!" Novak exclaimed, snatching the key ring from the deputy's hand. "Let's go!"

The two men raced to their horses and vaulted into the saddles. Seconds later they were galloping down the road, leaving Deputy Carlisle staring sheepishly after them from the doorway of the pharmacy.

"Oh, damn," the young man muttered as he looked

around and realized that he still did not have a horse. He looked left and right for a passing cab, but the street was empty. With a frustrated groan, he yanked the door shut behind him and sprinted down the road.

Inside the marshal's office, Alvin McNally and Benny Armatrading were going through the desks, searching for the keys to the cells in back. After the botched ambush at the rail yard, Armatrading had found McNally near the Orient Hotel, where McNally had just finished ransacking Nora Sutherland's room. Armatrading had informed him of Willie's death and Chris's arrest, and they had taken off at once, arriving at the jail in time to see Stuart Kennedy and the marshal riding away.

Guessing that the two men were on their way to the pharmacy, McNally looked through the window of the marshal's office and determined that only one deputy was on hand. He sent Armatrading to tie their horses around the corner, where they would not be seen, while he burst into the jail and blurted out that the marshal needed the deputy right away. The young man had been taken in completely and soon was running off down the street.

"Those keys aren't here," Armatrading insisted, dumping the contents of yet another desk drawer.

"Forget it," McNally said.

"What about Chris?"

"I'll take care of him. You keep guard out here."

McNally spun around and strode across the room. The door to the cellblock was unlocked, and he slipped through, closing it partway behind him. The area was lit by a pair of lanterns that hung at either end of the aisle between the four cells. The two forward cells were empty, while each of the far ones had a man lying on his cot.

"McNally? Is that you?" the man in the left cell asked as he sat up on the cot.

"Shut up!" McNally blared, nodding toward the stranger in the right cell, who sat up also and looked over at him questioningly.

Chris jumped to his feet and rushed up to the barred door of the cell. "Am I glad to see you! That fellow killed—"

"I know," McNally cut him off.

"Are you gonna get me out of here?"

"There's no key," McNally told him. "The deputy must've taken it."

"Then how are you gonna get me out?" Chris asked, his smile vanishing.

"Don't worry. I've got a plan." He glanced back at the tall man in the opposite cell, who looked as though he recently had taken a bad beating and still had a bandage over his broken nose. Then McNally leaned toward Chris and whispered, "Give me your pillow."

"What?" the young man said incredulously.

"Shh. Just give it to me." He nodded over his shoulder, indicating the other prisoner.

Chris seemed to realize what McNally was up to, for he smiled and then retrieved the pillow from the cot, handing it through the bars. He winked conspiratorially as McNally drew his revolver and slipped it behind the pillow to muffle the noise, all the while keeping his back to the man in the other cell.

Though Chris had no idea how Alvin McNally was going to get his cell door open, he had full faith in the gang leader, and he stood there grinning, waiting for McNally to turn and shoot the other prisoner so that there would be no witness to the escape. Instead, McNally said, "Sorry, Chris," and with only the slightest look of regret, he pulled the trigger.

There was a muffled roar, and the bullet slammed into Chris's chest, throwing him off his feet and against the far wall. As he slid to the floor, his smile turned to an expression of wonder. He looked down at the bloody hole in his chest, and then his eyes rolled back in his head and he fell onto his side.

The prisoner in the opposite cell jumped up, his face a mask of horror. He opened his mouth to speak, but the words caught in his throat as the big man turned toward him. A thin stream of smoke curled out a dark hole at the center of the pillow, which was pointed directly at him.

"No!" the man managed to gasp. "You . . . you don't have to. I . . . I won't tell. I swear—"

The word was cut off by a second and third muffled roar, the first bullet catching the man in the belly, the second in the chest. The man was knocked sideways off his feet, and he fell to the floor, twitched several times, and then lay motionless.

McNally heard a gasp behind him, and he swung the gun around, holding back at the last moment when he saw Benny Armatrading standing in the doorway. Armatrading was shaking his head in shock as he stared at the body of his comrade.

"It had to be done," McNally said flatly as he dropped the pillow to the floor and approached. "Eventually he would've talked."

Armatrading just stood there looking at Chris's body as McNally grabbed him by the sleeve.

"We've gotta get out of here," McNally said, pulling Armatrading around and forcing him from the cellblock. He practically dragged him through the office and out into the street.

"I . . . I'm all right," Armatrading told him as he took a deep breath of the cool evening air.

"Where are the horses?" McNally asked.

"This way." Armatrading led him around the corner and down a side street to where the horses were tied.

As they mounted up, McNally said, "We'd better split up. I'll go north, you south. We'll meet back at the hideout." When Armatrading did not immediately reply, he added, "You sure you're all right?"

Armatrading nodded numbly. Then he shook himself and declared, "I'm fine. I'll see you later at the hideout."

The two men kicked their horses into a gallop. They rode side by side for several blocks, and then with a parting wave, McNally peeled off to the north, while Armatrading turned his horse to the south.

The moment that Stuart Kennedy and Marshal Novak burst into the jail, they knew something was wrong. The door to the cellblock was ajar, and the unmistakable smell of gun smoke filled the air.

Novak cursed as he raced into the cellblock and saw the motionless, blood-covered bodies. Cursing again, he handed Kennedy the key ring and said, "I'll check outside." Then he turned and raced back through the office to see if he could find any trace of the murderer.

Kennedy fumbled with the keys until he found the one that opened the cell of the man who had ambushed him earlier that night. Entering, he quickly confirmed that the man was dead. He stepped across the aisle to the other cell, unlocked the door, and stepped inside.

The prisoner was lying motionless on his side, but Kennedy thought he detected a slight rise and fall of his chest. Kneeling beside him, he pressed against the man's neck and found a faint pulse. The man seemed to respond to the touch, for his eyes fluttered open, and he looked up at Kennedy. His lips quivered, as if he was trying to speak, and then he raised his head slightly.

Cradling the man in his arms, Kennedy urged him to lie quietly. The man kept struggling to speak, however, and Kennedy realized that allowing him to do so would not alter the inevitability of his death, so he said, "What is it?" and leaned his ear close to the man's lips.

"It . . . it's all his fault," the man suddenly blurted, his voice surprisingly strong.

"Who?" Kennedy asked. "Who did this to you?"

"The b-bastard got me f-fired," he sputtered. "All his fault."

"What are you talking about?"

The man reached up and clutched Kennedy's lapel. "Tell him he put me here. He murdered me!"

"Who did?"

The man's eyes started to roll back into unconsciousness, but then he jerked them open and said, "Jimmie boy. It's all his fault."

"Jim? Jim Hart?" Kennedy asked, suddenly realizing that this must be the editor who had attacked Hart on the street and was due to get out of jail the next day.

"That's the bastard."

"He shot you?" Kennedy said incredulously.

"He put me here. He . . . he might as well've pulled the trigger." The man started to cough, and a thin stream of blood bubbled out of the corner of his mouth.

"But who shot you?"

The man shook his head slowly, his eyes gazing into the distance. "Why did he have to send that second lead? I ran his first story word for word. If only I'd have run that new lead about those crewmen. . . ."

"Forget the story," Kennedy said. "Can you describe the man who shot you?"

"I'll never forget!" the man raged. "He always resented me. He sent that second lead to destroy me. And he's done it. He . . . he's killed me."

"What did the man look like—the one who pulled the trigger?" Kennedy pressed. "Tell me what he . . ." His voice trailed off as the man's head lolled to the side and his body went limp.

Kennedy again checked the man's pulse and confirmed that he was dead. He lowered the man's head to the floor, then stood and used the blanket on the cot to wipe the blood from his hands.

There were footsteps in the office, and Kennedy turned to see Marshal Novak coming through the doorway. "I couldn't find anyone," Novak told him.

"They're both dead," Kennedy replied, deciding that there was no reason to tell him that the editor had survived for a time. He pointed at the body at his feet and said, "This is that newspaper editor, isn't it?"

"Yes. Timothy Blaine."

"Did he have any family?" Kennedy asked as he stepped from the cell and followed Novak into the office.

"I don't think so. I guess *The Rocky Mountain News* was his family. I suppose I ought to let them know what happened."

"I'm planning to stop in at the newspaper office on my way back to the hotel and check out a few things about that first train wreck," Kennedy said. "I'll be glad to tell them, if you'd like."

"Like? I'd love it. That's one job I never mind passing along to someone else."

"Fine. One other thing, Marshal."

"Yes?"

"Is it possible for you to keep my name out of things for the time being?"

"No problem," Novak agreed. "And for now I'd rather not draw a connection between Harold Trimm's murder and those train collisions—publicly, that is. Likewise the murders here at the jail. The less the killer realizes we know, the better."

"Good idea." Kennedy started toward the front door. "I'll stop in later when your deputy's back for a description of the man who sent him on that wild goose chase."

"No need for that. I'll have him take a copy of his statement to your hotel later."

"Thanks," Kennedy replied, turning to leave.

"Kennedy," the marshal called. When the Faraday agent looked back, he continued, "You might as well use Deputy Carlisle's horse. He can pick it up when he goes to your hotel."

Kennedy thanked him again and departed.

Not two minutes later, while Novak was attending to the bodies in the cellblock, the front door burst open and Deputy Carlisle stumbled into the room, revolver in hand. He stood there, puffing and gasping for breath, wondering if he had missed any action.

"Put the gun away," Novak called from the cellblock doorway. "It's over."

"Did I miss something?" the younger man asked as he approached, craning his neck to look over Novak's shoulder.

"Sit down and catch your breath for a minute," the marshal told him, pointing to one of the desks. "We've got plenty of work to do, and then I've got a little errand I want you to run."

"Run?" Carlisle asked suspiciously.

"Over to the Orient Hotel. Anything wrong with that?" Novak asked with a grin as he turned and disappeared into the cellblock.

Chapter 8

"MY CHICKEN IS DELICIOUS," NORA SUTHERLAND EXCLAIMED, putting down her fork and looking up at Jim Hart, who was seated across from her at one of the tables in the dining room of the Orient Hotel. "How is your veal?"

Jim Hart was caught still chewing, but he managed to swallow it down in a big gulp before replying, "Excellent. And the vegetables are done with just the right touch of crispness." He started to cut another piece of meat, then paused and said, "It's a shame your brother couldn't join us. Did he say when he'd be back?"

"I expected him by now, but even when we were children Stuart would often get involved in some project of his and forget the time."

"Do you think he's over at the depot?"

"He had several errands to run. I'm sure he'll be along presently." Wishing to change the subject, she asked, "And how did your afternoon go?"

"I interviewed a number of people at the Union Pacific offices and at the rail yard, and then I transmitted a follow-up story on the latest collision."

"I was thinking more about your new-found celebrity."

Hart blushed. "It felt strange being interviewed by other reporters. I never expected that I would become part of the story."

"You won't be the first journalist to become famous," she pointed out.

"I have no desire to be famous—just respected."

"They often go hand in hand."

"Well, I'd rather let my stories speak for themselves."

Hart grew silent and looked down at his plate. Nora was about to speak, but she thought better of it and resumed her meal. After a few minutes, Hart looked up again and asked, "What do you really think of me, Nora?"

It was Nora's turn to look uncomfortable. Cautiously, she began, "You're very considerate, and I admire your tenacity and ability."

"What if I'm not all that I seem?"

Nora looked away. "None of us are really what we appear to be on the surface."

"Yes, but you're so genuine," he said. "I, on the other hand, am a caldron of inconsistencies. If you were able to see under the surface, you might not like—"

"Aren't you being too hard on yourself?" Nora asked. "We're all a bit insecure when it comes to ourselves."

"It . . . it's just that I really care what you think of me."

"I know," Nora replied in a near whisper. "I'm sorry."

"Please, don't be. Not on my account."

Nora leaned forward. "I want you to think of me as a friend. But I . . . I don't want it to go any further than that."

"Is it your husband?" Hart asked. Seeing her confused expression, he went on, "Your late husband. You never speak of him."

"I'm not ready to tell you about my husband," she said, her voice soft and distant.

"I'm sorry. I don't mean to pry, but if there's anything I can do . . ."

"Thank you, but there isn't. I'm just not able to talk about it now. Perhaps soon." She paused, then added, "I hope so."

The couple went back to eating in silence. They were interrupted a few minutes later by the arrival of the waiter, who came up to Jim Hart and said, "There is a gentleman to see you, sir."

"Who is it?" Hart asked. He glanced beyond the waiter toward the hotel lobby but saw no one.

"The gentleman did not give his name, but he said it was urgent. He is waiting in the front parlor just off the lobby. Shall I give him a message?"

"No, that's all right. I'll see to it myself."

"As you wish." The waiter bowed and withdrew.

Hart turned to Nora. "It's probably one of the reporters checking something on deadline. Would you mind—?"

"Of course not."

"I'll be as quick as I can." He started to rise, then nodded toward his meal, which was almost finished, and said, "You can let the busboy remove my plate. But I did have my eye on that almond torte on the dessert tray."

"There will be a slice waiting when you return," Nora said with a smile.

Hart rose and headed off into the lobby. Turning left, he crossed the room and entered the small front parlor. To his surprise it was empty. He stood there looking around, wondering where his visitor had gone, and was about to return to the dining room when the desk clerk came over and said, "Mr. Hart?"

"Yes?"

"Your guest asked me to tell you that he would be out back in the garden getting some air."

"I see," Hart replied, not really seeing at all. "Thank you."

Hart walked back through the lobby and down a short hall, at the end of which was a door that led to the Japanese-style garden out back. Opening the door, Hart stepped out into the cool evening air.

It was quite dark out, and it was difficult to make out the surroundings despite the little Oriental lanterns that were hanging from the dwarf trees along the walkways. The entire area seemed deserted, and again Hart considered returning to the dining room. But then a voice called his name, and he turned to the right to see a shadowed figure standing on one of the paths.

"Who is it?" Hart called, taking a few cautious steps toward the man.

"It's me," the man replied as he stepped forward into the light of one of the lanterns.

As soon as Jim Hart saw the red-checkered shirt, he guessed that it was the same man who had been looking in at him from the lobby during breakfast—the one who had caused him to lose his appetite. The man came fully into the light, and Hart recognized his thin physique and sharp, angular features.

"Benny?" he said incredulously. "What in God's name are you doing here?"

"I had to come," Benny Armatrading insisted, approaching along the walkway until the two men were standing face to face.

Hart scowled. "I told you never to ask for me at the hotel. What if someone saw us together and—?"

"I had to come, Mr. Hart. Something's happened."

"What is it?" Hart's tone was suddenly nervous.

"It's Alvin McNally. He . . . he just killed one of our own men. Over at the jail."

"Whatever for?"

"Didn't want him to talk. I . . . I'm scared. If he finds out I've been giving you information—"

"He's not going to find out," Hart cut in.

"But he's smart. He may figure out that someone told

you where those crewmen could be found after the first crash and how to find the place we ripped up the rails for the second crash."

"Listen, he's not going to find out," Hart repeated sternly. "I've been real careful to make those discoveries seem accidental, just like I promised. There's no reason for him to suspect that I knew anything beforehand."

"I don't like it," Armatrading muttered, shaking his head and frowning. "If you report something special after the next crash—"

"Then there's going to be another one?" Hart prodded.

"Well, yes. One final one, I think."

"Where? When?"

Armatrading shrugged. "We don't know. He hasn't told McNally yet."

"You still haven't told me who that man is."

"I don't know. Honest. McNally says he don't know the guy's name, either. All he cares is that the fellow has enough money to pay."

"Last time you said he was an older man."

"Yep. Sixty at least, with white hair and mustache. A little fellow. Drives a buggy."

"You're not holding back on me, are you?"

"I'd tell you if I knew," Armatrading insisted.

"Good. Now, I need to know when and where the next crash will take place."

"I just don't know." Armatrading looked down and kicked the dirt with the tip of his boot. "McNally killed Chris tonight. If he finds out that I've been selling information . . ."

Hart removed the billfold from his pocket. Pulling out a small wad of bills, he counted out one hundred dollars and held it out to Armatrading. "This is for you," he said. "Go on, take it."

Armatrading eyed the money for a moment, then snatched it away and stuffed it into his pants pocket.

"If you let me know where the next train wreck will

take place—before it happens—there's another two hundred in it for you."

"You aren't gonna turn me in, are you?"

"I'm a journalist. It's my responsibility to keep the public informed—not to capture the perpetrators," Hart said firmly, as if trying to convince himself of the propriety of what he was doing. "I just want to be there when it happens so that I can give my readers an eyewitness account."

Armatrading looked at him closely. "I . . . I just don't know."

Hart peeled off another bill and handed it to his informer. "Trust me," he told him. "Nothing is going to happen to you."

"And if something does happen . . . if the law catches us . . ."

"I'll make you a hero," Hart vowed. "I'll see to it that you never serve a day in prison."

"You promise?"

"I promise."

Armatrading stared at him for a long moment, and then finally he nodded. "I'll get word to you before it happens," he declared.

"Good." Hart clapped him on the shoulder. "Now get going. And don't ask for me in the hotel again. If you need me, catch me alone on the street—or if you must, sneak up to my room."

Armatrading nodded and started across the garden, away from the hotel.

"Benny," Hart called after him, and Armatrading halted and looked back at him. "What were you doing in the lobby this morning?"

"I . . . I was gonna tell you that there's only gonna be one more crash," Armatrading lied, not eager to tell the reporter that McNally was after Hart's two friends.

"That was foolish, coming to the hotel like that."

"I know. But I only had a few minutes in town." Armatrading glanced around nervously. "I gotta get back to the hideout before he gets suspicious." He turned and disappeared into the night.

For a long moment, Hart stared after him, deep in thought. So far this whole affair seemed so simple: a gang orchestrating the destruction of railroad property at the bidding of a mysterious wealthy man with the stipulation that no one be hurt. And until today no one had been seriously injured. The only murders connected with the case were of the two drifters in the boxcar, but apparently they killed each other before the crash.

Hart told himself that paying an informer merely helped ensure that he stayed a jump ahead of the competition. But now murder had become involved, and that changed the climate considerably. Then again, the man who died was part of a ruthless gang of outlaws—a gang that lived by the gun and could expect to die by it. Still, he wondered whether or not he should tell at least some of what he knew to the authorities—or perhaps Stuart Kennedy.

Hart shook off the thought. *One more train wreck,* he told himself. *One final collision. And when it's over, everyone will have heard of the name Jim Hart.*

Soon after Jim Hart headed out back to the Japanese garden to meet with his visitor, Stuart Kennedy entered the dining room and joined Nora at her table. Nora noticed at once that her partner looked not only perturbed but a bit disheveled, as well.

"Is something wrong?" she asked in an undertone as he took an empty seat beside her.

"Where's Jim?" he asked, glancing around.

"He was called away for a minute—one of his news friends, I believe."

Kennedy nodded. "I'm afraid things didn't go as planned," he began.

"Didn't that chemist come up with anything?"

"He's dead," Kennedy stated flatly.

"My God," she said, keeping her tone low. "How did it happen?"

"Somebody got to him. From the condition of his body, I'd say earlier this afternoon. He must have told them something, because I got ambushed on the way to the pharmacy." Seeing her concerned expression, he immediately raised a hand and added, "Don't worry, I'm all right. I had to kill one man, and a second got away. But I took one prisoner."

"Did he talk?" she asked enthusiastically.

"No. And I'm afraid he never will. Someone broke into the jail and killed him—along with that editor who attacked Jim Hart."

"Oh, no."

"It was probably the same person who killed the chemist."

"What are we going to do now?"

"I found a piece of glass, probably a shard from that fragment Harold Trimm was analyzing. I figured I'd send it to the lab in Kansas City on the night train."

"I'd like to send my film along for developing, also," Nora told him.

"Good idea."

"I'll have to ask Jim where he wants copies of the prints sent."

Kennedy narrowed his eyes slightly and leaned toward her. "About Jim Hart . . ."

"Yes? What is it?"

"You like him, don't you?"

"Well, yes . . . as a friend, of course."

"Has he said much about his work to you?"

"Well, not really. How do you mean?"

"I'm not trying to insinuate anything," Kennedy said hesitantly. "I mean, I know he's an aggressive reporter and all. But he's had a string of remarkable luck with those stories about the crashes."

"What are you implying?" she asked, raising one eyebrow skeptically.

"You must admit he's managed to be in the right place at the right time."

"Along with a dozen other reporters," Nora pointed out. "He's just been more careful and thorough. You know how important that is in our business, too."

"Yes, I suppose so. But I turned up a curious bit of information tonight over at *The Rocky Mountain News*, which makes me question exactly how he's getting his information. It seems—"

"Just a minute," she cut him off with a wave. "Here he comes."

Kennedy nodded. "We'll talk about it later."

Jim Hart looked deep in thought as he approached through the dining room. Upon reaching the table, however, he smiled broadly and said, "I'm glad you could join us, Stuart." Sitting down, he turned to Nora. "I'm sorry about the interruption. It was one of the boys from the *Post* checking some facts for the morning edition."

"About yesterday's train collision?"

"Yes, of course," Hart replied, looking surprised at the question. Glancing down, he saw that the almond torte had been served while he was gone, and he picked up his fork and smiled at Nora in thanks.

"I was just wondering if they had heard about the murders," Kennedy said almost casually.

"Murders?" Hart dropped the fork. "What murders?"

"Four of them. One at the rail yard, two at the marshal's office, and a druggist over on Larimer Street."

"You're kidding." Hart's mouth gaped open as he stared back and forth between Nora and Kennedy.

"I wish I were."

"What exactly happened?"

"Do you want the real story—or the one Marshal Novak is going to give you?"

"The real one, of course."

"It has to be off the record; we don't want to prematurely tell the perpetrator what we know. For the moment you'll have to go with the marshal's account that the murders are unrelated and that none of them are connected to the train collisions."

"Then there is a connection—with all four of them?"

"Do you agree to keep it off the record for now?"

"Yes, I do," Hart stated emphatically.

With Hart's assurance to keep the information confidential, Kennedy recounted the day's events, starting with his visit to the pharmacy that afternoon. He apologized for not having told Hart about the fragment of glass earlier but assured him that he would have filled him in the moment there was any concrete evidence. He went on to describe being ambushed that evening and the murders at the jail. He concluded by informing Hart that his former managing editor had been slain also, though he made no mention of Blaine's final words.

"Timothy Blaine . . . murdered," Hart said numbly. "I just can't believe it." He shook his head and sighed. "It makes no sense at all."

"Murder rarely does," Kennedy commented. "Especially when you're dealing with someone who places no value on human life."

"But that's what makes no sense."

"What do you mean?" Nora asked.

Hart looked first at Kennedy, then Nora. "Whoever carried out those train collisions made a real effort not to hurt the crew. Then he—or they—turns around and murders the druggist, his own partner, and an innocent newsman who just happens to be in the next cell. And from what you're saying, he probably killed those drifters, as well."

"He has a point there," Nora told Kennedy.

"Yes, there are still a lot of loose ends and inconsistencies," Kennedy admitted. "Maybe they never intended to kill anyone but now are running scared. A scared animal is a dangerous and unpredictable one."

Hart sat in quiet contemplation for a moment. Then he looked up at his companions and announced, "I really should head over to the marshal's office and take his official statement, then telegraph out a story."

"By the way," Kennedy said, "Marshal Novak has agreed to keep my name out of things for the time being."

"Don't worry, I won't mention you, either. Just don't forget that I want to be on hand when you finally close in on the killer."

"You can count on it."

"Thanks." Hart stood and smiled at Nora. "Thank you for ordering the dessert, but I think I'll forgo it this evening. Perhaps tomorrow."

Nora nodded that she understood, and Hart took his leave. As he walked from the dining room, he stopped at the desk of the maître d'hôtel and arranged to have the dinner bill charged to his room, then exited through the lobby.

After Jim Hart had departed, Nora suggested that Kennedy order some dinner, but he explained that the events of the evening had left him without an appetite. Together they left the dining room and headed upstairs.

As Nora was reaching for the doorknob to her room, she pulled back and called Kennedy over. "I think someone's been inside," she whispered, pointing to the floor.

Kennedy looked down and saw that the sliver of paper she had closed between the door and the jamb was now lying on the floor. He quickly checked his door and said, "Mine wasn't disturbed." As he came back over, he drew his Smith & Wesson and held it at the ready. "Let's not take any chances," he whispered, and Nora nodded and took out a small pocket revolver from her purse.

Kennedy tested the doorknob and discovered that it was unlocked. Signaling Nora to stand to one side of the door, he did likewise on the other side. Then he reached over, turned the knob, and thrust the door open. When there was no sound from within, he crouched down and darted into the room. Behind him, Nora stepped into the doorway and aimed her gun toward the center of the room.

Nora had left an oil lamp burning low on one of the tables, and it cast just enough light for them to see that the entire room was in disarray. Cautiously Kennedy circled the room, yanking open the wardrobe door and checking behind the floor-length draperies. Satisfied that the intruder was no longer there, he relaxed somewhat and raised the flame on the lamp, then closed the door.

"Just look at this mess," Nora exclaimed, turning in place in the center of the room. Virtually all of her belongings had been emptied from the wardrobe and dresser and lay scattered on the floor or draped haphazardly across the bed.

"Can you figure out what they were after?" Kennedy asked as Nora began sorting through her things.

It took several minutes for her to discover the answer, which came when she lifted one of her dresses from the floor near the corner of the room. "I think I've got it," she declared.

Kennedy came up beside her and looked down at the floor. There in a crushed heap were the remains of Nora's camera. The film leader was still attached to the spool, but the rest of the roll had been torn off and was missing.

"Somebody must have wanted those pictures very badly," Kennedy commented.

Nora shook her head. "If he wanted the pictures, he wouldn't have exposed the film," she pointed out. "No, he didn't want them. He just wanted to make sure we didn't have them, either."

"What could have been so incriminating in them?" Kennedy asked. "And I wonder how someone found out you were taking pictures in the first place."

"Maybe the pictures will give us an idea."

"If only we could put our hands on them," Kennedy said glumly.

"Simple," she declared, smiling at Kennedy's quizzical expression. "Do you recall my saying that I wanted to send the film to headquarters for developing? Well, I had already prepared to do just that." She crossed to the bed, where she had tossed her purse. Opening it, she withdrew a small wrapped package. "The film," she said, holding it aloft. "What they destroyed was a new, unexposed roll."

"You're fantastic!" Kennedy exclaimed, coming over and giving Nora a hug. "But I thought you had to send the whole camera back to the lab?"

"I used to. But the last time Matthew Faraday sent back the camera loaded with fresh film, he included a couple of unexposed rolls and directions on how to load and unload it myself. He figured it might increase security and speed up the process."

"It looks like he was right. How come you never told me?"

"I know we've been together for almost a year now, but a woman has to keep a few secrets—even from her partner," she teased. "That's why I like to handle the photography myself. If you ever learn how to do it, you might decide you don't need me anymore."

"Never!" he proclaimed, kissing her cheek.

"Ah, well," she sighed. "It looks like tonight I may have to risk divulging a few of those secrets."

"What do you mean?" he asked.

"Tell me . . . when you were in Harold Trimm's laboratory, did you happen to see any hydroquinone or pyrogallol? One of the thiosulphates would be nice, too—sodium or ammonium."

"What in heaven's name are you talking about?"

"I'm talking about you and me trying to figure out what might be on these pictures that would induce someone to tear my room apart. I'm talking about developing this film ourselves, rather than taking the time to send it all the way to Kansas City."

"You can do that?" he asked incredulously.

"I can do anything, my dear," she said coyly, "provided Mr. Trimm was nice enough to stock the right chemicals."

"Well, I can't swear there's any of that hydro-whatever-you-said. But he seems to have had every other chemical in the book."

"Come on, then. Let's find out."

Nora searched the piles of clothing until she found her evening shawl. Then she and Kennedy locked up the room and made their way downstairs. Deciding that they did not want to have a cabbie waiting out in the street while they broke into Trimm's pharmacy, they arranged with the hotel management to rent a buggy for the evening.

The Faraday agents parked their buggy in front of the pharmacy on Larimer Street and entered Harold Trimm's laboratory through the alley door. After lighting a couple of lanterns, Kennedy cleaned off the right-hand worktable while Nora set about gathering the chemicals she would need to develop the film. Finding them all in good supply, she commented that Trimm must have been a student of photography, which she pointed out was one of the current frontiers of chemical research.

Soon Nora had lined up a number of bottles of chemicals, including hydroquinone, sodium thiosulphate, sulphite, and acetic acid.

"See if you can find a pair of scissors," Nora said as she inspected a number of flat metal pans on a shelf and chose three. "I have to prepare the developer and fixer."

A few minutes later, Kennedy returned with a large pair of scissors from the counter in the store. "Anything else I can do?" he asked as he watched her mixing chemicals in two of the pans.

Nora handed the third pan to Kennedy. "Could you

fill this with water?" She nodded toward a small sink off to one side. "About half full."

Kennedy brought the pan to the sink and filled it from the hand pump. Returning, he placed it on the worktable beside the others. "What's all that for?" he asked, indicating the other two pans.

Nora pointed to the first. "This is a solution of hydroquinone. It's the developer."

"What does that mean?"

"Basically, the film is coated with a compound containing silver halide crystals. When it's exposed to light by opening the shutter of the camera, the crystals react and undergo an invisible change—the more light, the greater the change. The developer"—she pointed to the first pan—"converts the exposed silver halide to metallic silver. The more exposure a section of film receives, the greater the amount of the metallic silver that forms. That's why the film is called a negative, because the brightest areas turn to silver, which appears black. The unexposed sections remain the invisible silver halide."

"What about that pan?" Kennedy pointed to the second one, in which Nora was currently mixing a number of chemicals.

"This is the fixer. It contains the thiosulphate, sulphite, and acetic acid."

"You're confusing me," he said, shaking his head.

"It's simple. After developing, there's still a lot of silver halide in the film—the sections that didn't turn to metallic silver. The trick is to remove those crystals before they react with light. The thiosulphate does that. It fixes the image in place, which is why it's called the fixer."

"What about the other chemicals?"

"When the film is transferred to the fixer, some of the developing liquid mixes in, and this can cause stains on the negative. The sulphite and acetic acid counteract the developer. Don't ask me how. I'm no chemist; I just know how to do it."

"And the water?" He pointed to the pan he had brought over.

"That washes away the developer and fixer." She stood away from the pans and wiped her hands on a towel. "It's time to prepare the film. Turn off the lanterns, please."

"How will you see what you're doing?" he protested.

"I'll have to rely on the moonlight. If any other lights are on, the film would be exposed again, and all the pictures would come out black."

As Kennedy turned down the lanterns, Nora opened her purse and took out the package containing the exposed roll of film. Once the room was dark, she opened the package, removed the heavy black paper surrounding the film, and placed the roll on the counter.

"We're very lucky this isn't a year ago," she commented.

"What do you mean?"

"When the Kodak was introduced, the film consisted of a strip of paper coated with gelatin that contained the silver compound. After it was developed, it had to be stripped from the paper and pressed against a piece of clear gelatin to create the negative. That was a very delicate operation, and I wouldn't have had the supplies and equipment to carry it out. Just this year they introduced this new film, which uses clear nitrocellulose rather than paper, so that the film itself becomes the negative."

As Nora spoke, she used the scissors to cut the film into strips holding six pictures each. Once the strips were prepared, she laid them in the developing solution and waited a few minutes. Every so often she used a pair of tongs to lift out one of the strips and check the progress of the development. When she was satisfied with the quality, she removed each strip and laid it in the fixing bath, stirring them around to help remove the excess silver halide crystals. Next she transferred each strip to the pan of water, which she refilled several times to ensure that all the chemicals were washed away. Finally, after the water was wiped off and the strips were laid out on towels to dry, she told Kennedy that it was all right to relight the lanterns.

"We won't be able to create prints," she said as she picked up one of the strips. "That requires using a special camera and photographic paper to take a picture of the negative, which reverses the dark areas to light and vice versa. But this should do."

She held the strip to the light of the lantern and began examining each round negative. When she finished with the strip, she handed it to Kennedy to examine and started on the second.

It was on the third strip that Nora said, "I may have something here."

"What?"

"Take a look at this picture." She handed him the strip. "It's the third one down."

"What about it?" he asked, examining the negative.

"See that big fellow on the left? I took this shot without his knowing. When I then asked the two of them to pose for a shot, he not only refused, he walked away."

"Strange. Where exactly was this taken?"

"On the westbound train, right at the spot where the last derailed car was connected to the first boxcar that stayed on the tracks."

"That's right near the one with the bodies of the drifters," Kennedy noted. "If he was hanging around there, he would know that I was examining the bodies, which might explain why I was followed and ambushed —and why Harold Trimm was killed."

"And if he realized I took this picture—and if he's involved with those train wrecks—he'd obviously want to destroy the film."

Suddenly Kennedy snapped his fingers. "The deputy said that it was a big man who rushed into the jail and told him the marshal wanted him—just prior to the murders in the cellblock." He stared at the negative again. "This could be our man."

"What will we do?"

"Well, for now he probably feels a little safer thinking that the film is destroyed. I suggest we go along with our original plan and put these negatives on the night train to Kansas City, along with the piece of glass. It's only a six hundred mile journey—it will get there by morning. We'll have the lab make prints and try to figure out the identity of this man—and anyone else, for that matter."

"On the way we ought to stop at the marshal's office to see if that deputy recognizes this fellow in the negative," Nora suggested.

"Good idea. As a matter of fact, he was going to bring me a full description, but we left the hotel before he showed up."

Gathering up the negatives, they turned off the lanterns and headed out to their buggy.

"It's been a long day," Nora commented as they started down the street toward the marshal's office. "It will be good to get to bed."

"I've been meaning to discuss that with you," Kennedy said, snapping the reins. "I'm thinking of skipping bed tonight."

"What do you mean?"

"I mentioned visiting *The Rocky Mountain News* earlier. Well, a small inconsistency turned up regarding that first collision, and I'd like to go back to Greeley to check it out.

"Tonight?" she asked in surprise.

"There's a late train to Cheyenne. I'd only need a few hours in Greeley, and I could catch a morning train back. I'd be here by noon."

"Do you really think it's important?"

"It could be."

Eyeing him in the moonlight, Nora read the grim determination in his pale-blue eyes. Placing a hand on his forearm, she said, "Perhaps you'd better tell me exactly what this is all about."

Chapter 9

"HOLD UP, THERE!" THE GUNMAN SHOUTED AS HE STEPPED from the shadows into the thin moonlight and leveled his Winchester repeating rifle at the buggy, which had slowed up upon approaching the copse of trees.

Edward Trenary pulled his buggy to a halt. "I've business with Mr. McNally," he called in reply.

The gunman took a step closer and eyed the white-haired man in the dark business suit. Though he did not know the man's name, the gunman recognized him as the one who was funding their recent escapades, so he lowered the muzzle of the Winchester and waved him into an opening in the trees.

Trenary drove the buggy through and approached the ramshackle pair of cabins that served as the current hideout for the McNally gang. Situated near the train tracks some fifteen miles northeast of Denver, it allowed easy access to both the rail lines and the city.

As the elderly man climbed out of the buggy, Alvin McNally appeared in the doorway of the smaller shack. He grinned upon seeing his visitor and waved him inside. The shack contained little more than a table and chairs and four bunks, with some pegs on the wall for coats, hats, and holstered revolvers. Seated at the table playing cards were two men, one of them McNally's right-hand man, Benny Armatrading; the rest of the gang had accommodations in the larger cabin.

"What is it?" McNally asked as he followed Trenary into the lantern-lit shack. His smile faded when he saw the man's grim expression.

"I'll get right to the point," Trenary declared, paying no attention to the presence of the two cardplayers as he wheeled around to confront McNally. "Word is spreading through Denver about a shoot-out at the rail yard and a double murder at the marshal's office. What do you know about it?"

"Why should I know anything?" McNally asked, narrowing his eyes.

"Come on, McNally. It doesn't take a genius to figure out that you were involved. The question is why."

"Look, I don't have to explain anything to you," McNally said bitterly. "You paid me to do a job, and I've been doing it—just like you asked. None of the crewmen got hurt on any of those trains."

"I said I didn't want *anyone* hurt—not just the crewmen. I'm beginning to think that those drifters didn't kill each other but were helped to their graves."

"They saw us ripping up the track," McNally said in an even tone, making no attempt to deny the allegation. "They could've identified us."

"So you killed them?" Trenary balled his fists as he stared up at the bigger man, who was at least a head taller. "Murder wasn't part of our bargain," he said through clenched teeth.

"Maybe it's not what you bargained for, but you've been fooling yourself if you thought we could get away with a scam this big without somebody getting hurt."

"Damn!" Trenary blurted, pounding a fist into his palm. He turned and paced across the room, then stood gazing through a dirt-grimed window into the darkness outside. "It wasn't supposed to be like this."

"Stop worrying," McNally said in a surprisingly gentle tone. "You had nothing to do with those killings. I did it to protect my men; it's my neck that's on the line. There's nothing to implicate you. Hell, you've never even told me your name."

Trenary spun around, his expression livid as he sputtered, "You . . . you ruined everything! The whole point was to create an air of mystery surrounding those train collisions. Now it's become little more than a series of dirty crimes."

"Look, mister," McNally said, losing his patience. "I don't care what your motives are. You hired me to do a job, and I've done it. But I don't intend to let myself or my men get caught or killed in the process."

Trenary gave an abrupt, bitter laugh. "You seem to be doing a good job of that yourself. Two of your men are dead already—isn't that right?"

McNally scowled. "They knew the risks going in."

"Well, maybe the risks have gotten too high."

"What do you mean?"

"I'm not so sure we should continue with this thing anymore," Trenary said flatly.

"Look, there's no call to back out now," McNally said defensively. It was clear from his expression that he was concerned about losing the money that another train collision would bring the gang. "Those other incidents couldn't be helped. The drifters saw us, and then some fool insurance investigator got a line on that chemical you gave us to use."

"So you tried to kill him?"

"He got one of my men, instead."

"Good for him," Trenary lashed back, folding his arms across his chest. He glowered at the other two men, who remained seated at their table, pretending to be playing a game of poker.

"Look, there's no call for—"

"Now you listen to me," Trenary lashed back, stabbing a thumb at the bigger man. "I came out here to call off this whole thing—but I'm going to give you one more chance. But only on one condition: No one gets killed. That includes the insurance investigator. If you get rid of him, they'll just bring in someone else." He paused a moment, allowing the words to sink in. "Are you agreed?"

McNally nodded.

"Good. In that case there'll be one more collision, and then I suggest that you and your men get out of the territory for a while." Trenary pulled an envelope from his coat pocket. "You'll find half the money in there. I'll bring the other half when the job's done . . . provided you don't kill anyone."

McNally reached out and took the envelope. He did not bother to open it but tossed it onto one of the bunks.

"Remember," Trenary continued. "If anyone gets murdered—if anything happens to that insurance man, for instance—you don't see another cent."

"Don't worry," McNally grunted. "We'll do it your way."

"See that you do."

Pulling a map from his pocket, Trenary walked over to the table. As he started to unfold it, the two men gathered their cards and rose from their seats.

"Here's where it's to be done," Trenary said, spreading the map out on the table.

McNally walked over and looked at the spot where Trenary was pointing. "But that's the same place as the last crash," he said in bewilderment.

"Precisely. The first two collisions were in completely different locations. They won't be expecting lightning to strike in the same place again."

"You want it carried out the same way as last time?" McNally asked.

"Yes, with two exceptions. First, I want the eastbound train shunted this time, instead of the westbound. And since that reporter figured out how you did it last time, there's no need to return the tracks to their original condition when you're done."

"All the better," McNally said, smiling. "When's it to take place?"

"Tomorrow night. The eastbound will be coming through at twelve thirty. The westbound arrives ten minutes later."

"I'll have men on each train."

"Have you got enough ether?" Trenary asked.

"Six bottles left. We should only need four."

"Good. Get rid of the rest when you're done." He folded up the map and stuffed it back in his pocket, then started across the room.

"Can I ask you one thing?" McNally called as the old man reached the door.

Trenary turned and eyed him suspiciously.

"What's this all about?" McNally continued. "I mean, why do you want those trains destroyed?"

"That's *my* business," Trenary replied coldly. "Just see that you don't make any mistakes."

Trenary opened the door and stepped out into the darkness. Though the moon was nearly full, a bank of high-level clouds reduced the light considerably, so that it was difficult to see the surrounding countryside.

Turning back in the doorway, Trenary said, "It's getting darker out. I had a hard-enough time finding my way out here before those clouds came overhead. How about sending one of your men to ride ahead of my buggy and guide the way?"

"No problem." McNally glanced over at the two men who were standing beside the table. "Turner, saddle up and—"

"I'll go," Benny Armatrading interjected, coming forward from the table. "I could use some air."

McNally eyed him curiously, then shrugged and said, "If you want, go ahead."

Armatrading grabbed his holster from a peg beside one

of the bunks and buckled it around his waist. Snatching up his coat and hat, he strode from the shack and started saddling his horse.

"Don't get any ideas about spending any time with one of those fillies at Meg's place," McNally called to him from the doorway. "You can have your fill of whoring when this job is done. I want you back on the double."

"Sure thing, boss." Armatrading swung into the saddle and led his horse over to where Edward Trenary was seated in the buggy. "Just follow me," he called to the elderly man. Then he kneed the horse and started forward through the trees.

As soon as the buggy and rider had disappeared into the darkness, McNally went back into the shack. He started to close the door, then stood staring out for a moment.

"Turner," he called abruptly, spinning around toward the other man, who was lying on one of the bunks. "Why do you think Benny was so eager to go?"

"Who knows?" Turner replied.

"It's funny. He just got back from Denver a while ago—and after all the excitement in town, I'd have thought he'd be ready to hit the sack."

"Guess he wanted some air, like he said."

"I don't know." McNally started across the room, then stopped in place. "I want you to follow him, Turner, and make sure he comes right back. If not, find out what he's up to and then get back here."

Turner gave a long sigh but did not voice any objection. Standing, he gathered his things and headed from the cabin.

"Make sure he doesn't see you," McNally called after him. Then he shut the cabin door and walked over to his bunk. Without bothering to remove his boots, he stretched out full length on the bed. Five minutes later, he was sound asleep.

* * *

It was well after midnight when Jim Hart returned to the Orient Hotel. His evening had been unusually busy after leaving Nora Sutherland and Stuart Kennedy at the hotel dining room—an evening that had begun with a visit to the marshal's office, where he found himself to be one of several reporters on hand to take a statement about the recent murders. Afterward he had written a story about the murders and telegraphed it to the eastern newspapers that had been running his accounts of the train collisions.

As Hart approached the hotel entrance, a voice called his name from behind. Spinning around, Hart saw someone standing in a darkened doorway directly across the street.

"It's me," the man called in a loud whisper. "Benny."

Hart glanced around to make sure no one was watching. Then he quickly crossed the street to where Benny Armatrading was standing.

"What do you want?" he asked in concern.

"I only got a minute," Armatrading began. "It's about that fellow in the buggy—the one who hired us to crash them trains."

"What about him?"

"He rode out to the hideout. I just finished leading him back into town."

"What did he want?" Hart pressed.

Armatrading looked around nervously. "If McNally finds out I came here . . ."

"He won't find out. Now, you're already here, so you might as well tell me what's going on." Hart drew out his billfold and counted out several bills. "Go on," he prodded, pushing the money into Armatrading's hand. "What did you come to tell me?"

"Well, that fellow hired us for one last crash, like I told you he was gonna."

"Do you know when?"

"Tomorrow night—at the same spot as the last crash."

"Are you certain?"

"That's what he said," Armatrading replied, his tone defensive. "He figured no one would expect that."

"What time?"

"We're gonna hit the eastbound freight train that comes through at twelve thirty and the westbound ten minutes later."

"You're sure of all this?" Hart asked again.

"That's what the man said," Armatrading insisted. "Only this time we're gonna shunt the eastbound train."

"All right." Hart handed Armatrading another bill. "Thanks."

"Are you gonna be there?" Armatrading asked.

"I'm not sure. But listen . . . if something should happen, if anything goes wrong, you just get yourself out of there."

"Don't worry," Armatrading replied as he folded the money and shoved it into his coat pocket. He glanced around furtively, then said, "I really gotta go. McNally expects me back."

As Armatrading turned to leave, Hart grabbed his arm. "Benny. Are you sure you don't know the name of that man in the buggy?"

"Haven't a clue."

"What about McNally?"

"He don't know either."

"All right." Hart released the man's arm. "Good luck, Benny."

"You, too," Armatrading replied. He headed down the street and rounded the corner.

A moment later, Hart heard the hoofbeats of a horse fading into the distance. Pulling up his coat collar, he crossed the street and entered the hotel.

"Jim," a woman called, startling Hart as he stepped into the lobby. "It's Nora."

Hart turned to find Nora Sutherland seated in a chair near the window of the parlor just off the lobby. "Whatever are you doing up?" he asked.

"I couldn't sleep," she said, standing as he approached.

"What's the trouble?" He led her over to the sofa and sat beside her. "Has something happened?"

"No, nothing like that," she reassured him. "I'm just concerned about Stuart—after this evening's attack."

"I'm sure he'll be fine." Hart patted her hand reassuringly.

"I know, but I don't like it when he's away like this."

"Away? What do you mean?"

"Oh, yes, he didn't tell you. He decided to ride up to the site of the first collision so that he can clear up some loose ends."

"What loose ends?" Hart asked.

"Oh, I don't know. His reports are always very thorough, and I suppose there are a few things that need straightening out."

"How long will he be gone?"

"I expect him back in the morning."

"I'm sure everything is fine," he assured her. "He wouldn't want you to be sitting up all night worrying about him."

"I suppose not."

"Then why not let me escort you to your room? We can meet in the morning for breakfast, if you'd like." Again he patted her hand, and this time he left it resting there.

"Yes, I'd like that." She smiled, but then her expression grew more serious, and she pulled her hand away. "I don't mean to pry, Jim, but may I ask you something?"

"Of course. Anything."

"I wasn't spying, but I was sitting over there by the window, and I happened to see you speaking with that man. He didn't look very reputable to me."

Hart grinned, though it was an awkward one. "I shouldn't expect so. He's little more than a common thief."

"An outlaw?" she said in surprise.

"Not really. But I'd say he lives only just this side of the law."

"Whatever did he want with you?"

"I'm a journalist, remember? I have to maintain contacts with all sorts of people."

"Was it something to do with the murders?" she asked.

"Sort of. I asked him earlier to see if he could find out what the talk is on the street. Perhaps we could get a line on the perpetrator that way."

"And . . . ?"

"I'm afraid he turned up nothing. No one seems to have any idea who's behind it all." Hart stood and held out his hand. "Enough idle chatter," he proclaimed. "I'd say it's time you got some rest."

Standing, Nora took Hart's arm and allowed herself to be led up the stairway to her room on the third floor. When they reached her door, she took out her key and slipped it into the lock. She started to turn the knob, then paused and turned to him. Their eyes met, and for a moment it appeared as though Hart was about to take her in his arms and kiss her. But then Nora averted her eyes and pushed open the door.

"Thank you," she said, looking back at him and smiling.

"For what?"

"For being considerate."

"There are times when I wish I weren't so considerate."

"I know," she whispered. Leaning toward him, she kissed him lightly on the cheek, then quickly backed through the doorway and closed the door.

For a long time Jim Hart just stood there staring at the closed door, wishing he had swept her into his arms. Then with a sigh, he turned and walked away down the hall.

It was still several hours before dawn when Benny Armatrading passed the man on lookout and rode up to the hideout used by the McNally gang. As he dismounted in front of the smaller cabin and unsaddled his horse, he did not notice that Turner's horse stood saddled near the other building and that it had been ridden hard.

As Armatrading tossed the saddle over the porch rail, the cabin door opened and Alvin McNally stepped out, still dressed and smoking a cigarette.

"I thought you'd be asleep," Armatrading said, walking past him and entering the cabin. He looked around at the empty bunks. "Where's Turner?" he asked.

"I sent him over to the other cabin," McNally replied, following Armatrading inside and closing the door behind him. "He snores too loud."

As Armatrading hung up his coat and hat and removed his holster, he forced a grin and said, "We made it to Denver all right, but it really did get dark. I practically had to pull that buggy out of several ditches."

"Did you, now?" McNally walked over to the table. "Sit down a minute, Benny," he said, pulling out one of the chairs and holding it for the other man.

Looking a bit bewildered, Benny came over and sat down. "What's wrong, boss?" he asked, looking awkwardly over his shoulder at the big man, who still stood behind the chair.

"I was going to ask you the same thing," McNally said, dropping his cigarette to the floor and stepping on it. "Don't you like working for me anymore?" he asked, coming around the chair and staring down at Armatrading.

"I . . . of course I do."

"Then why have you started working for that young reporter fellow?"

Armatrading instinctively looked away. "What are you talking about?"

"That's who that fellow was outside the Orient Hotel, wasn't it?"

"I don't know what you're talking about." Armatrading shifted uncomfortably in the chair.

"I think you do." McNally's smile was gone as he bent over, placed both hands on the arms of Armatrading's chair, and stared him in the face.

"Really, I don't," Armatrading blustered with as much conviction as he could summon.

"Don't lie to me," McNally grated. "I had Turner follow you. He saw you meet with that reporter fellow in front of the hotel. Then after you left, he looked through the window and saw the reporter sitting with that camera lady of his. Turner rode hard to circle ahead of you and get back first." McNally stood up straight and grinned ominously. "So don't try to lie to me, boy."

"You . . . you don't understand."

"Help me understand, then." McNally stood there, arms across his chest, waiting for Armatrading's explanation.

"I—I didn't say nothing. I swear," the smaller man stammered.

"The hell you didn't!" Without warning, McNally lashed out, backhanding Armatrading across the face.

Grabbing his cheek more in surprise than pain, Armatrading started to shake his head. "Really, boss. He was trying to blackmail me—about the murders—but I refused to tell him anything."

This time McNally struck him with a fist that sent him reeling backward over the chair. Armatrading shook his head to clear it but made no effort to stand as McNally tossed aside the chair and stood over him, blaring, "You went there on your own—and Turner saw you pocketing money!" Suddenly he stooped down, grabbed hold of Armatrading's coat, and tore away the pocket. Several large bills fell to the floor. "I want to know exactly what you told him! Now!"

When Armatrading did not respond, McNally bent down and dragged him to his feet. The smaller man raised his arms to protect his face, but McNally unleashed a vicious blow to the belly instead, doubling him over. It was followed by a knee to the face, snapping back his head. Twisting his collar and lifting him upright, McNally slapped him several times, then threw another right cross that knocked him back against the wall.

As Armatrading slumped to the floor, McNally drew his revolver. Aiming it at Armatrading's head, he said, "This is your last chance. Tell me what that reporter knows."

"I . . . I didn't mean to. . . ." Armatrading began, raising a hand to his bloody, broken nose. "He . . . he just wanted to know enough to stay ahead of the other newsmen."

"Is that how he came up with those stories?" McNally demanded.

"Yeah. He doesn't want to turn us in, just—"

Armatrading's words were cut off abruptly as McNally kicked him in the belly, knocking him over onto his side. "You little bastard!" he raged. "You sold us out for . . . for what? A few extra dollars?" He bent down and grabbed Armatrading's collar again. Raising a fist, he said, "You tell me what he knows, or I'll kill you! So help me, I'll kill you!"

Armatrading feebly raised his hands to ward off any blows. "He . . . he just wants to be there when the crash takes place."

"You told him, didn't you?"

Armatrading looked down and nodded weakly.

"You damn fool," McNally said in a bitter whisper.

"He won't tell anyone. You gotta believe me," Armatrading pleaded. "He just wants to be there so he can write a story afterward."

"He'll have his story," McNally said coldly, standing and backing away. "But it'll be his epitaph."

Crossing to the front door, McNally threw it open and looked outside. Several men were gathered in front of the other cabin, waiting to see what McNally would do to the traitor in their midst.

"Drag this scum out of here," McNally blurted, walking away from the cabin to where his horse was tethered. "Then saddle up—everybody. We've got business to attend to before sunup."

Half an hour later, Alvin McNally and his men were riding in the predawn darkness along the tracks of the Union Pacific Railroad.

Benny Armatrading had a good idea of what was coming. He had long since given up trying to protest—the cloth jammed into his mouth and tied in place with a bandanna made any such attempt feeble at best. He could do nothing but sit there feeling his body going numb, partly from the tight ropes that lashed his wrists to the saddle, partly from the shock of knowing that he soon would be dead.

"Over there, boys!" McNally called as he spurred his horse toward a small wooden trestle that traversed a narrow creek.

Armatrading almost lost his already-precarious balance as his horse began to gallop with the others toward the shallow embankment that led down to the dry creekbed. He wondered why he bothered to hold on to the saddle horn. He might as well let go, slip from the saddle, and get dragged by his wrists under the animal's pounding hooves. Yet there was something in him that would not give in—some vain thread of hope. Or perhaps it was just a macabre curiosity about how the end would come.

McNally pulled his men to a halt directly underneath the trestle, where they could not be seen from above. Guiding his horse close beside Armatrading's, he pulled a bowie knife from his boot and cut free the bindings at Armatrading's wrists, not caring that the big blade was slashing the man's flesh in the process.

"Get him down off there," he demanded.

Several men quickly dismounted and dragged Armatrading from the saddle, pinning his bloody hands at his sides.

"Now we wait," McNally intoned as he and the rest of the men dismounted.

They did not have long to wait, for several minutes later they heard the low rumble of a train approaching from the same direction they had come. As the sound grew louder and the trestle began to vibrate, Armatrading became increasingly frantic, until it took nearly all the men to restrain him, while a couple of men held the reins of the horses and kept them calm.

"Pick him up," McNally ordered as the train thundered closer.

The men grabbed Armatrading's arms and legs and lifted him off his feet, holding him with his back to the ground. He began kicking and twisting wildly, but with a couple of men at each arm and leg, there was nothing he could do but squirm. He was screaming, but beneath the gag it was little more than a piteous moan.

McNally scrambled up the embankment and took a quick look at the approaching train. It was a long freight train with at least forty or more cars.

Sliding back down to where the men were holding Armatrading, he leaned close to the terrified man's face and shook his head. "You shouldn't have talked, Benny," he said in an almost fatherly tone.

The crescendo built until the trestle beams were noticeably shaking. And then suddenly the engine roared overhead, followed by the tender and boxcars.

McNally again drew his bowie knife, this time holding it close to Armatrading's neck. "You'd like me to make it quick for you, wouldn't you?" he asked, pressing the blade against his throat. But then he released the pressure and slashed upward, cutting away the bandanna. He grabbed at the gag in Armatrading's mouth and yanked it out.

"Go on, scream if you want!" McNally shouted above the din of the train overhead, but Armatrading was stunned into silence. Looking up at the other men, McNally said, "Let's get him up there."

Tightening their grips, the men carried Armatrading up the embankment. The train was still rumbling by, with the caboose not yet in sight.

"Take a good look at it!" McNally yelled into Armatrading's ear as his men angled his head downward, so that he was looking upside down at the endless line of wheels streaming by. "Take a good look! And pray!" He burst into laughter.

"N-no," Armatrading stammered, his eyes widening in horror. "P-please, don't!" And then he began to shout, "No! No! No!" until the words became a single wailing scream.

"Do it!" McNally shouted at his men.

In unison, they swung Armatrading away from the train, then threw him headlong onto the rails between two of the boxcars. The scream cut off abruptly as Armatrading was swallowed up beneath the grinding wheels, his body ripped apart as it was sent bounding along the track.

McNally stood watching for a moment, as if mesmerized by the spinning wheels. Then he shook himself out of his reverie and signaled his men to hurry down the embankment before the caboose came by. They scrambled back to their horses and stood holding the reins until the entire train had passed overhead and receded into the distance.

Suddenly McNally's horse reared up, and he had to yank hard on the reins to keep it in place. Then a second horse tried to pull away, its eyes bulging with fright.

It was then that McNally saw the blood dripping from above and striking the horses. He looked up through the trestle ties and saw what remained of Benny Armatrading's body lying in a heap just overhead.

"Let's get out of here," he said, leading his horse out from under the trestle—away from the smell of death.

Chapter 10

AT NINE O'CLOCK THE NEXT MORNING, JIM HART HAD FIN-
ished dressing and was preparing to go upstairs to Nora's
room to see if she was ready for breakfast. Closing the
door to the bedroom, he stood in the front sitting room
of the suite, checking his billfold to make sure that he
still had enough cash after having paid Benny
Armatrading for the information about the upcoming
train collision. As he was pocketing the billfold, there
was a knock on the hall door.

"Yes?" he asked, approaching the door.

"It's Nora," a voice called on the other side.

Thrilled that she had come looking for him, Hart
swung open the door and was about to speak when he
saw that Nora was not alone. "Stuart," he said, taken
aback. "I thought you would still be at Greeley."

"It took less time than I thought, and I was able to
catch the early-morning train back," Kennedy explained.

"Have you eaten yet?" Hart asked him. "Nora was
going to have breakfast with me, and we'd love to have

you join us." Seeing that the two of them looked particularly somber, he turned to Nora and said, "Is something wrong? Are we still having breakfast."

"Do you mind if we come in?" she asked, forcing a smile.

"Of course not." He backed from the door and motioned them to enter.

Kennedy and Nora walked into the sitting room, and Hart closed the door behind them.

"Won't you sit down?" he asked, indicating the pair of upholstered chairs that along with a writing desk comprised the furnishings of the small room. "I'm sorry it isn't more spacious," he added, taking up a position near the desk as they sat down.

"No, this is very nice," Kennedy commented, looking around. "I didn't realize you had a suite."

"It's really not much more than the regular rooms." He gave a casual shrug. "I find it useful, since it also has to serve as my office."

"Of course," Kennedy said.

The three of them grew silent for a few moments, until finally Hart asked, "Am I mistaken, or is there something on your mind? Has something happened?"

Nora looked at Kennedy uncomfortably, then turned to Hart. "Jim, I think you'd want us to be completely frank with you."

"Of course. What is it?"

"Stuart has uncovered some confusing information."

"In Greeley, I take it. What is it?"

"I won't mince words." Kennedy leaned forward in the chair. "I believe you have been holding back critical information regarding these train collisions."

Hart shook his head nervously. "Whatever are you talking about?"

"I first became suspicious yesterday evening, when Timothy Blaine was shot. What I didn't tell you is that he spoke to me before he died."

"I don't understand." Hart shrugged as he looked back

and forth between Nora and Kennedy.

"I would've thought he'd want to tell me who shot him. But he seemed more interested in talking about you."

"He blamed me for getting fired—and also for getting locked up."

"I know," Kennedy continued. "But something he said struck me as strange. He mentioned that he had run your first story about the train crash and had merely left off the second lead you filed later."

"I still don't see what you're getting at."

"In effect, he was saying that you telegraphed an account of that first train wreck and subsequently transmitted a new lead for that story." Kennedy stood and walked a few feet away. With his back to Hart, he went on, "I figured he was confused. He was near death after all. So I went over to the newspaper office and checked up on it. Sure enough, several people recalled receiving a complete story at about the same time the other reporters would have been telegraphing theirs. A second telegram had the new lead about the discovery of the missing crewmen. It was received a couple of hours later—around the time we arrived in Greeley." Kennedy turned and fixed Hart with a steady gaze.

"There's a simple explanation," Hart said with an awkward smile. "I had no idea that we would find those crewmen, and I wanted to make sure that my newspaper didn't miss out on the initial story. So I paid someone to send that first account while I stayed behind with you at the crash site."

"I know you did," Kennedy said without the trace of a smile. "I confirmed that this morning. In fact, the person you paid was one of the drivers of the buckboards that took those reporters into town. The telegraph operator remembered it quite well, because you had included some extra money to make sure that he transmitted your story before those of the other reporters."

"Precisely."

"Jim," Nora said, standing and walking over to him. "You didn't have time to write that story before those buckboards pulled out. Think about it. One of us was with you the entire time."

"I . . . I don't know what to say." Hart awkwardly shifted on his feet.

Nora placed a hand on his forearm. "We don't want to think badly of you, but there really is only one conclusion we can draw." When Hart just stood there looking pale, she continued, "You knew about that collision before it even took place, didn't you?"

Kennedy stepped closer now. "You had the original story already written before we reached the scene. You were so afraid of being beaten by the competition that you had that story all prepared and had someone else send it out as soon as you were certain the collision had taken place. Meanwhile, you remained behind to get a new angle that the others didn't have. It was a slight risk, but of course you had no reason to suspect anyone would take notice. And you never dreamed that your editor would refuse to run the new lead."

Hart just stood there, looking numbly from one to the other, his lower lip trembling.

"That isn't all, is it?" Kennedy went on. "The reason you stayed behind is because you already knew where to find those crewmen. That's how you were able to lead me right to them."

Hart's shoulders sagged. He staggered over to one of the chairs and slumped into it, then buried his face in his hands. "I . . . I'm sorry," he mumbled.

"I'm afraid I haven't been entirely honest with you either, Jim," Kennedy said. "I'm not an insurance investigator for the railroad."

Lowering his hands, Hart looked up at him questioningly.

Nora came over and sat in the other chair. Leaning toward Hart, she said softly, "My brother is an agent for the Faraday Security Service. He's been investigating this case for the railroad."

"You're . . . you're a Faraday man?" Hart asked, and Kennedy nodded.

"You must tell Stuart how you knew in advance about that crash," Nora went on. "And how you knew where those rails had been tampered with during the second crash."

"People have been murdered," Kennedy said coldly. "Whoever is behind this must be stopped."

"Jim, I'm going to ask you something, and I want you to promise to be truthful." Nora's tone was so gentle and compelling that Hart looked up at her and nodded. "Jim," she went on cautiously, "are you a part of it? Are you somehow involved?"

"Good God, no!" Hart blurted. His expression grew more agitated, and he looked anxiously from Nora to Kennedy. "You've got to believe me," he pleaded.

"We want to," Nora assured him. "But you must tell us exactly how you found everything out."

Nodding, Hart sagged a bit deeper in the chair and stared down at the floor. Nora and Kennedy waited silently until he was ready to speak. Finally he began, "I'm a reporter—and a damn good one. And a reporter has to rely on confidential sources. It goes with the territory."

As Hart spoke, his voice slowly grew stronger and more assured.

"One of my contacts was a two-bit crook who had a friend in a gang that had begun operating in this region. My contact was a bit disgruntled when they wouldn't let him into the gang, so he told me that he heard from his friend that the gang was on to a big scheme—something to do with train collisions. I had nothing solid to go on, but I used the information from the first source to track down his friend in the gang. Then I convinced that gang member to talk—partly with money and partly with assurances that I could help him out if the gang ever got arrested."

Hart sighed. He started to look up at Nora, then turned away as if embarrassed.

"Anyway," he continued, "this new source fed me information about both train wrecks and enabled me to get the angles I needed to stay out in front on the stories."

"Why didn't you just go to the authorities—before the crashes even took place?" Nora asked.

Hart looked at her as if the answer was obvious. "I'm a reporter, not a lawman . . . or a Faraday agent." He glanced over at Kennedy. "It's my job to report the news, not influence it."

"Weren't you influencing the news when you paid off that informer?" Kennedy asked. "And when you unveiled secrets of the mysterious collisions? Who knows how you may have affected events? For all you know, what you did might have been partly responsible for pushing that gang into murder."

"It's my responsibility to report the news," Hart argued. "To keep the public informed—any way I can." He turned to Nora, his expression almost pleading for understanding. "If I hadn't paid off that informer, those crashes would have taken place anyway. The only difference is that the public would not have been as well informed."

"I'm sorry," Nora said, shaking her head. "I just don't see it that way. If you had reported what you discovered to the law, this whole thing might have been averted. And you still would have had an exclusive story—just a slightly different one."

"There's no point arguing about this any longer," Kennedy proclaimed. "We can't change what happened before. The important thing is what we can do about the future."

Suddenly Nora exclaimed, "It was that man last night!

He's your informer, isn't he?" When Hart nodded, she started to ask the man's identity, but Kennedy signaled her to let the question lie.

"How did they do it?" Kennedy asked. "What did they use to knock out the crewmen?"

"Some kind of gas. He didn't know the name of the chemical, just that it's a clear liquid packed in round flasks and that it turns to a gas when the bottle breaks."

"And now I want you to tell me the name of the people carrying this thing out," Kennedy said firmly.

"The gang is run by a fellow named Alvin McNally. He's supposedly a big brute of a man—probably the killer you're looking for."

"There was a big man working at the rail yard," Kennedy told him. "Nora took a photograph of him at the second crash site—which is why he came after us yesterday. Last night the deputy recognized the man in the picture as the same one who sent him off on a wild goose chase just before the murders at the jail. And when the train pulled in this morning, I checked with the rail yard and found out that he hasn't shown up at work since the day they cleared the tracks."

"He must be McNally, then."

"Most likely," Kennedy agreed.

"Why is he doing it?" Nora asked. "What's in it for him?"

"Money," Hart said evenly.

"But the railroad finally determined that nothing was ever taken from the trains," Nora pointed out.

"From what my source tells me, McNally's gang is being paid by someone else—a wealthy old man with white hair and mustache who drives a buggy. Unfortunately, I have no idea who he is. Supposedly McNally doesn't even know."

"Just great," Kennedy said facetiously. He circled the room, coming to a stop at the far side. Turning back toward Hart, he said bluntly, "Is there going to be another collision, Jim?"

When Hart hesitated, Nora grasped his arm and said, "You've got to tell us."

"They've resorted to murder," Kennedy added. "If they have to, they'll do it again."

"I know," Hart said, looking down again. "Yes, there is going to be one final wreck. My informer told me—" He stopped himself short.

"Go on," Nora encouraged. "What did he say."

"What will you do if I tell you?" Hart asked Kennedy.

"He has to be stopped."

"I understand. But how will you go about it?"

Kennedy paused a moment, deep in thought. Then he replied, "I'll arrange with Marshal Novak to have men hidden aboard both of the trains. We can catch them in the act and round up the whole gang together."

"What about the man who hired them?"

"The important thing now is to forestall that crash. Perhaps afterward, through McNally, we can capture whoever's behind it."

"Where will it take place?" Nora asked. "And when?"

"I want to be on that train with you," Hart said flatly.

"You're crazy," Kennedy shot back. "You're lucky if the marshal doesn't lock you up for—"

"I'll either be on that train with you—or I'll be there alone."

"Out of the question."

"Then get your own informer and figure out where and when." He gave Kennedy a smug grin.

"This is blackmail," Kennedy said, narrowing one eye.

"I call it good journalism," Hart retorted. "You may be right—I may have acted imprudently in the past. But I'm not about to sit by and let the story of a lifetime slip away from me."

"I don't know. . . ." Kennedy said, unconvinced.

"Remember our deal," Hart reminded him. "You said you'd let me be there when—"

"You broke any deal we had when you held back vital information."

"Then let's make a new deal. I tell you where and when; you let me go along and get the story first-hand."

"You really don't know when to quit," Kennedy said, grinning for the first time.

"I'm tenacious, remember?"

"I won't be responsible should something happen to you," Kennedy warned him.

"And I'll leave your name out of the story if you still want me to."

"I don't know why I'm doing this." Kennedy shook his head in wonderment. "But all right. You can come. Just don't get in the way."

"You won't even know I'm there," Hart assured him.

"So when is the collision supposed to take place?" Kennedy asked, taking out a pencil and pad to write down the information.

By late afternoon, plans were in place for Stuart Kennedy and Marshal Sam Novak to hide aboard the eastbound train later that night with a contingent of deputies, so that they could catch the bulk of the McNally gang in the act of shunting the train onto the opposite track. The marshal reluctantly agreed to allow Jim Hart aboard as an observer. Several other men were to be stationed on the westbound train to capture the gang members assigned to take it over.

At four o'clock, Stuart Kennedy left the hotel and headed to the telegraph office to contact the Faraday agency. He wanted to see what progress they were making with the evidence they should have received that morning. Again he arranged with the office manager to use the equipment, and soon he was seated at the key tapping out the codes that were required to patch him directly to the telegraph operator at Faraday headquarters in Kansas City.

As soon as Kennedy made the connection and gave the appropriate password to prove his identity, he was given authorization to proceed. He decided against transmitting in secret code and began:

SENT PACKAGE FOR ARRIVAL THIS MORNING STOP PLEASE VERIFY RECEIPT STOP SK

By ending with his initials, Kennedy signaled the other telegrapher to proceed. He then pulled over a pencil and pad and began to translate the return message:

PACKAGE ARRIVED STOP CONTENTS INCLUDE NEGATIVES FOR PRINTING AND IDENTIFICATION AND ONE PIECE GLASS FOR ANALYSIS STOP HOLD FOR REPORT STOP FSS

There was a two-minute delay, and then the message from FSS—Faraday Security Service—resumed.

GLASS FRAGMENT ANALYZED STOP COATED WITH TRACES OF DIETHYL ETHER STOP CLEAR TOXIC CHEMICAL WITH PUNGENT BURNING ODOR STOP TURNS TO INVISIBLE GAS ON CONTACT WITH AIR BUT DISSIPATES RAPIDLY STOP FORMERLY USED AS ANESTHETIC STOP CAPABLE OF RENDERING UNCONSCIOUS FOR SEVERAL HOURS ANYONE WHO INHALES FUMES STOP FSS

HAVE YOU IDENTIFIED BIG MAN IN PICTURE INDICATED STOP SK

SO FAR UNABLE STOP IDENTIFICATION PROCEEDING STOP FSS

CHECK WANTED GANG LEADER ALVIN MCNALLY FOR POSSIBLE MATCH STOP SK

HOLD FOR ADDITIONAL INFORMATION STOP FSS

There was another long pause. When the message resumed, it came somewhat slower and less precisely, and Kennedy realized at once that someone else was at the key.

IMPORTANT NEW INFORMATION STOP LAB HAS CHECKED DIETHYL ETHER MANUFAC-TURERS STOP ONE IN CHICAGO SHIPPED CASE OF CHEMICAL TO DENVER ONE MONTH AGO STOP NAME OF RECIPIENT EDWARD TRENARY STOP DO YOU KNOW TRENARY STOP MF

From the closing signature, Kennedy knew that the man on the other end was now Matthew Faraday himself.

DO NOT KNOW STOP DO YOU HAVE DE-SCRIPTION OR BACKGROUND STOP SK

INFORMATION SKETCHY STOP NEW YORKER WHO INHERITED GREAT WEALTH STOP LIVES IN SECLUSION AND DROPPED OUT OF SIGHT IN PAST YEAR STOP THOUGHT TO HAVE LEFT COUNTRY STOP MF

DO YOU HAVE DESCRIPTION STOP SK

HAVE PHOTO IN FILE STOP BEING SENT TO YOU STOP PLEASE HOLD STOP MF

This delay was far shorter. When the message re-sumed, Kennedy could tell that it was still Matthew

Faraday on the other end, but he was obviously excited because he was transmitting at a pace that was almost too fast for his abilities.

NORA HAS SEEN TRENARY STOP SHE TOOK PICTURE OF HIM AT SITE OF TRAIN CRASH STOP OPERATOR WILL TRANSMIT DETAILS STOP MF

While the regular operator replaced Matthew Faraday at the controls, Kennedy waited with pencil in hand, wondering if this Edward Trenary might have taken some kind of a railroad job that put him at the scene of the accident during the cleanup and resulted in his accidentally ending up in one of Nora's pictures. Or perhaps he and Alvin McNally were one and the same man. After all, the only proof so far that there was an old man in a buggy was the word of Jim Hart's outlaw informer.

A moment later the message from the regular operator resumed, and Kennedy had to write quickly to keep up with him. When the man gave his ending signature, Kennedy stared down at what he had written, uncertain at first whether he had gotten it correctly. Then he took hold of the telegraph key and transmitted:

UNDERSTAND INFORMATION STOP WILL TAKE IMMEDIATE ACTION STOP WILL SEND FULL REPORT TOMORROW STOP SK

Kennedy briefly considered telling headquarters about the coming operation that night, but he did not want to take a chance on someone's overhearing or intercepting his message and word getting out about their plan. Instead he gave the final sign-off signal and ended the transmission.

After thanking the Western Union manager for his

cooperation, Kennedy hurried from the telegraph office and took a cab back to the hotel. He went straight to Nora's room and knocked on the door.

"What is it?" she asked, opening the door and seeing Kennedy's harried expression.

"We have to talk." He stalked into the room and started to pace. "I received some new information from the agency—it may change things."

"What do you mean?" she asked.

"First, does anyone know that you're a Faraday agent?"

"Of course not."

"What about Jim Hart? He knows I'm an agent. You haven't told him—"

"No. We agreed I'd continue pretending to be your sister."

"Good," Kennedy said, breathing a sigh of relief. "It's important that no one yet know the truth."

"They'll find out soon enough when I appear on that train tonight," she commented.

"I don't want you on the train," he said firmly.

"Now Stuart, if we're going to work as a team, you can't try to protect me from—"

"It has nothing to do with protecting you. It's just that there's another job that needs doing—and you're the only one who can handle it."

Nora eyed him curiously. She had seen that expression on his face before, and she knew it always meant something exciting—and dangerous—was about to take place.

It was dark out, and all the hall lamps had been lit as Nora Sutherland made her way downstairs to Jim Hart's room on the second floor. She knocked and waited for him to answer. When the door finally swung open, she said, "Stuart asked me to see if you are ready."

"Yes, just about. Please come in." He stepped back, and she entered the small sitting room.

"Are you sure you want to be there tonight?" she asked as he took a coat from the desk chair and put it on.

"Of course."

"It may be dangerous."

"This could be the story of a lifetime. There's no way I'm going to miss out on it." He came over and took her hands. "Don't worry about me. I'll keep my head down."

"Just do what my brother tells you to. He knows how to handle these things."

"I will," he assured her. "And what about you? What will you do tonight?"

"Probably sit up in the lobby and worry."

"I'd tell you not to, but I know it would be useless." He smiled at her. "If you're determined to worry, then I might as well give you one more thing to worry about." He leaned forward to kiss her, but at the last moment she turned her head slightly so that his lips only touched her cheek.

Nora pulled back and turned away slightly. "I . . . I know how you feel, Jim. But we're different, you and I."

"That's what adds the spice."

"We see things differently. For instance, the way you handled that information about the trains."

"I made a mistake," he admitted as he came around her and again took one of her hands in his own. "I've learned my lesson."

"Have you?" she asked, looking up at him. "Are you certain?"

"Yes," he said with conviction. "I told your brother everything I know, didn't I?"

"I have no idea. Did you?"

"You were there," he replied a bit testily.

"For all I know, you may not have told us any more than you had to."

"You don't really think that about me, do you?" he said, looking noticeably perturbed.

"I don't know what to think anymore."

"Then stop thinking—stop worrying." He smiled

again, though without as much confidence. "Wait until this thing is all over. Then you'll see that I've changed."

Nora reached up and touched his cheek. "I like you, Jim. I *do* want us to be friends."

"And we are," he interjected.

"If there's anything you want to tell me—any way I can be of help . . ."

"Everything is going to be fine, Nora. You'll see."

Nora looked down and nodded, forcing a faint smile.

"That's better," Hart told her. He walked over and opened the door. "We'd better get going, before I miss the train."

He ushered Nora into the hall and locked the door behind him. As they started down the hall, they were met by Stuart Kennedy, who had just come from his room.

"Nora," he said as he came up to them. "You forgot your key." He handed her a room key, which she clutched in her hand. Kennedy then turned to Jim Hart. "Are you sure you're ready for this?" he asked.

"Lead the way," Hart proclaimed, raising his arm and pointing down the hall.

"I think I'll go to my room," Nora announced as they reached the stairs that led down to the lobby.

"Good-bye," Kennedy said, kissing her.

"You both be careful now," she admonished.

"We'll be back soon," Hart assured her. Taking her hand, he raised it to his lips. Then he turned and followed Kennedy down the stairs.

Nora stood alone at the top of the stairs, watching as the two men reached the lobby and headed toward the front door. She waited until they had passed through and disappeared into the night. Then she looked down at the key in her hand and sadly shook her head.

Nora did not like what she was about to do, but she knew that she had no other option. She had given Jim Hart one final chance to divulge everything he knew about the train collisions, but he had insisted that he had been totally forthright. Yet there still were elements that did not add up, and Stuart Kennedy had charged Nora with the task of trying to put the final pieces of the puzzle together. It seemed increasingly likely that the young reporter knew more than he was letting on, and it was just possible that in his room Nora might discover the extent of his knowledge and in the process unravel the mysteries that continued to plague this case.

Clutching the key more tightly, Nora returned to Jim Hart's door. As she slipped the key into the lock, she prayed that Kennedy had managed to sneak away the proper duplicate key from the front desk. She turned the key and heard the rasp of sliding metal, and then the lock opened.

Nora glanced quickly up and down the hall, making sure that no one was watching. Then she pushed open the door and slipped inside, shutting the door behind her.

Chapter 11

STUART KENNEDY AND MARSHAL SAM NOVAK SPENT MORE
than two hours in a warehouse near the rail yard meeting
with Jim Hart and the fourteen men who had been
deputized to carry out the night's mission aboard the
eastbound freight train. Novak had also arranged for
another contingent of deputies to be organized at Limon,
east of the intended crash site, so that they could ride
aboard the westbound train and arrest whomever
McNally assigned to gas the crew and take over that
locomotive.

Since there was a chance that one or two of McNally's
men might sneak aboard the freight train before it pulled
out of Denver, all of the deputies had to be hidden
aboard the train well before the scheduled departure
time of eleven o'clock. After Kennedy and Novak were
satisfied that everyone knew what he was supposed to
do, the group left the warehouse and took up their
positions on the train.

Six of the deputies, along with Jim Hart, were hidden

in the front boxcar, with an equal number accompanying
half a dozen saddled horses in a closed livestock car right
behind it. This second group of men would be responsible for going after any gang member who tried to escape
on horseback. The two remaining deputies were positioned at the rear of the train, just in front of the
caboose, where they would disarm and arrest the person
McNally sent to gas the crewman. There was no
crewman in the caboose, his position being taken by a
stuffed dummy that was left lying under the covers on the
bunk where the crewman rested during long journeys.

For this run, the train had been reduced in size to only
a dozen cars. Though the fireman's job was being taken
by Marshal Novak, it was impossible to replace the
engineer, so a volunteer had been chosen for the dangerous task. Stuart Kennedy, meanwhile, took a place in the
open-topped coal tender, from where he could look back
over the boxcar roofs and view the entire train.

At last eleven o'clock came around, and the train
pulled slowly out of the yard. The engineer matched his
speed with that of a longer freight train, so that they
would not reach the rendezvous ahead of schedule.

There was one stop in Aurora, just outside Denver,
where the train usually took on additional cars. Tonight
no cars were added, though the train remained at the
yard for the twenty minutes the operation generally
required. Finally the locomotive whistle blared, and the
train resumed its journey east toward the site of the most
recent collision.

As Stuart Kennedy sat at the top of the tender, he
continually scanned the surrounding countryside, illuminated by the cool blue light of the waning harvest
moon, which had risen into a perfectly clear sky. He
looked back at the line of cars and wondered when and
how the attack would come. Though it was possible that
someone had snuck aboard before the train had departed
from Denver, he thought the notion unlikely and guessed

that the ambushers would appear on horseback somewhere well before the place where the train was to be
shunted onto the westbound track.

Kennedy had just finished checking his pocket watch
when the riders appeared from off to the side, some five
miles west of Box Elder Creek. He ducked lower in the
coal tender and peered over the side. As the riders gained
ground and closed in on the train, Kennedy counted
three of them. He scrambled to the front of the tender
and called down to Novak and the engineer that the
ambush was on, then returned to his position.

As the riders reached the caboose, one man tossed his
reins to a second man and stepped expertly from his
horse to the rear vestibule. Kennedy guessed that momentarily he would toss the flask of ether into the
compartment and would enter a minute later, after the
gas had had time to dissipate. He would be surprised to
find himself face to face with the guns of two of Novak's
best deputies, who would be watching the entire operation from a small viewing window cut into the car just
ahead of the caboose.

As the two remaining riders moved forward alongside
the train, Kennedy had to duck into the hiding place he
had prepared in the coal tender back at the rail yard. It
consisted of a large crate buried under the coal in the
corner of the car. As soon as he was positioned inside
with his revolver drawn and a Winchester rifle at the
ready, he pulled the cover over the crate, reached
through the slats, and piled enough coal on top to render
the hiding place all but invisible in the moonlight.

Crouched in the darkness of the crate, Kennedy imag-
ined the movements being made by the two remaining
riders. As before, one man would hand his reins to the
other, whose job it would be to bring all the horses to
where the rest of the gang was ripping up and connecting
the tracks. The first man would then leap onto the ladder
that led to the roof of the boxcar immediately behind the
tender. Gaining the top, he would jump to the tender

and proceed forward until he was directly over the open cab of the locomotive. It would then be a simple matter to toss down the bottle of ether and incapacitate the crew.

Less than a minute later, Kennedy peered through the slats and saw his man at the edge of the boxcar roof. The fellow was a hulking shadow against the moonlit sky. He leaped across the three-foot gap between the cars and scrambled into the tender. As the man passed within feet of the buried crate, Kennedy drew in his breath in surprise. It was the man in the photograph—Alvin McNally.

McNally had a leather satchel slung over his shoulder, and as he crouched down and made his way across the piled coal to the front of the car, he opened it and carefully removed a glass flask. Kennedy saw pieces of some sort of cloth wadding fall from the satchel, and he guessed the bag was stuffed to protect the flask.

The big man cradled the bottle against his chest as he stepped up to the front wall of the tender and stood, with the wall about waist high. He looked down for a moment, and then he raised his hand and tossed the flask at the floor of the cab. Immediately he turned and retreated several feet, ducking back down again.

Even above the roar of the train, Kennedy could hear the muffled crash of the bottle breaking. He started counting to himself, wondering how long before McNally felt the gas would have dissipated enough for him to proceed.

McNally waited only about a minute, and then he stood and returned to the front of the car. He stared into the cab, apparently convincing himself that the two men were lying unconscious on the floor. At last he climbed over the side and disappeared down the ladder.

Kennedy cautiously removed the top of the crate but remained inside. The train continued at its present pace for several more minutes as it neared the site where McNally's men would be at work. Finally there was one short blast of the whistle, and the train began to slow. A few minutes later, it came to a complete halt.

Kennedy slipped out of his hiding place and crawled over to the side of the tender. He hazarded a look over the side and saw at least half a dozen men gathered around the train tracks ahead. He ducked down quickly as McNally jumped from the locomotive and started barking orders.

"I want this whole train searched!" he yelled. "Benny said that reporter would be on board, and I want him found!"

Kennedy knew that the deputies would not act until he or Marshal Novak gave the signal. As he glanced back over the side and saw the gang members drawing their guns and approaching the train, he decided to let them get as far as the first boxcar. Then he would fire the first shot, and the doors would slide open to reveal a surprise for McNally and his men.

Moving to the front of the car, Kennedy looked down and saw Novak and the engineer lying on the floor. Novak's face was toward the tender, and Kennedy saw him wink. Apparently the plan had worked; Novak and the engineer had managed to hold their breath long enough for the ether to dissipate.

As McNally's men went running past the locomotive toward the first boxcar in line, Kennedy ducked back down and waited until he thought they would be almost to the doors. Then he abruptly stood, raised his Winchester, and fired into the air.

The outlaws froze in midstep and spun around to see where the shot had come from. McNally had been walking back toward the locomotive, and he was the first to see the rifleman atop the tender.

"Hold it right there, McNally!" Kennedy shouted as he levered another cartridge into the chamber and aimed the rifle at the big man on the ground.

The boxcar doors were swinging open now, and the

gang members found themselves facing half a dozen armed men. Pandemonium broke out, with some of the outlaws trying to run, while others dropped to the ground and opened fire.

A bullet from one of the outlaws ricocheted off the tender, and Kennedy had to duck, giving McNally a chance to make his move. The big man drew his revolver and ran toward the locomotive, only to find himself facing the gun of Marshal Novak, who had jumped to his feet when the firing started.

McNally fired wildly as he leaped to his right and dove at the ground. His bullet caught Novak in the thigh, dropping him to his knees. The marshal managed to fire back, but McNally had disappeared from sight toward the front of the locomotive.

Stuart Kennedy was already scrambling down from the tender. He could hear the thundering of hooves as the remaining deputies emerged from the livestock car on horseback, their mounts leaping from the open door to the ground. The gunfire was already waning, and he knew that the element of surprise had assured them a quick victory.

Kennedy knelt down to check Novak's condition, but the engineer was already tending to the marshal, who signaled Kennedy to go after McNally. Kennedy jumped from the locomotive, rifle in hand, and rolled. A bullet whined past him as he came up in a crouch. Peering into the darkness, he caught sight of a figure running toward a horse that was standing some distance from the tracks.

Turning to signal one of the mounted deputies to go after McNally, Kennedy saw that they were all occupied rounding up the last of the fleeing outlaws. But one horse was running free; the deputy had either dismounted or been shot from the saddle. Gauging the distance, Kennedy ran at an angle to intercept the animal. He caught up to it just as it was passing and managed to grab hold of the reins and drag the horse to a halt.

Leaping onto the back of the horse, Kennedy kicked it into a gallop toward where Alvin McNally was just climbing into the saddle of his horse. He quickly overtook the outlaw leader, and as McNally started forward, Kennedy leaped from the back of his mount and flew full force into the big man. They both went tumbling off the horse, and as they slammed into the ground, Kennedy heard the crunch of glass breaking. Realizing that McNally had been carrying a second bottle of ether in the satchel at his side, Kennedy took a gulp of air and rolled away.

McNally, his eyes wide with rage, did not seem to realize what had happened. He scrambled to his feet and started to lunge at his attacker. Suddenly he staggered, shook his head as if disoriented, and fell facedown on the dirt.

Still holding his breath, Kennedy rose and kicked the big man to make sure he was unconscious. Then he walked back toward the locomotive, at last exhaling and taking a few deep breaths of air.

Kennedy saw that all resistance had ended, with the deputies gathering McNally's men in a circle and finishing the task of disarming them. As he continued toward where Marshal Novak was seated at the edge of the locomotive platform, Jim Hart came running up to him, waving a pencil and pad and grinning with delight.

"Incredible!" he shouted as he slapped Kennedy on the back. "They'll never believe this! It'll make every front page across America!"

Suddenly Hart turned toward the carriage road that paralleled the train tracks. Noticing his movement, Kennedy spun around and saw a buggy racing across the open field toward the train.

"What the—?" Hart muttered, looking confused.

As the buggy drew closer, the driver became visible: an elderly looking man with white hair and mustache, dressed in a business suit. He kept driving closer, apparently unaware of what had taken place.

"That's him!" Kennedy shouted, drawing the Smith & Wesson from his shoulder holster. He reached over and briefly grasped Hart's arm. "The man who hired McNally!"

"But how . . . ?"

Hart's words trailed off when the man in the buggy seemed to realize what had happened and started to turn the vehicle in a circle.

"Halt!" Kennedy shouted, raising his gun and taking a few steps forward. "Stop! Or I'll shoot!"

Rather than stopping, the man stood from the seat and slapped the reins all the harder, yanking them to the left so that the buggy would come around and he could make his escape.

"Stop!" Kennedy shouted a final time. And then he aimed his gun and began to squeeze the trigger.

Just behind him, Jim Hart stood transfixed by the scene. Suddenly he realized that Kennedy was going to shoot, and with a shout he lunged at the Faraday agent's arm. But the gun went off first, and as Hart barreled into Kennedy and knocked it from his hand, the man in the buggy clutched his chest and tumbled over the side of the vehicle.

Hart stumbled and dropped to one knee. Reaching toward the body of the old man lying facedown in the dirt fifty feet away, he staggered to his feet and started toward it. "That's not him," he muttered, his voice rising as he shouted, "You shot the wrong man!"

Kennedy ran up behind Hart and grabbed at his arm. "It's Edward Trenary," he declared, pulling him back. "It's the man who hired McNally."

"No!" Hart screamed, turning toward Kennedy and yanking his arm free.

Hart spun around and ran toward the body. Dropping to his knees, he rolled the man onto his side, all the while pleading, "Don't die! Dear God, don't let him die!"

A red stain was spreading across the white shirtfront

and dripping onto the dry dirt. The man's soft-green eyes stared up vacantly at the night sky.

"Don't die!" Hart continued to plead as he gently lifted the man's head from the ground.

As Hart cradled the man's head in his arms, the gray wig fell away, and a cascade of brunette hair tumbled out. Hart jerked in surprise. Then he stared more closely and reached for the mustache. It pulled away in his hand, revealing the delicate features of a woman.

"Nora?" he said incredulously.

Kennedy was standing over him, and seeing Nora's face, he gasped, "My God! I—I killed her!"

"Your . . . your sister . . ." Hart stammered. "What was she doing? Why was she dressed like this?"

"She's not my sister," Kennedy said numbly, looking down at her. "She's a Faraday agent, like me. She must have disguised herself like this to try to fool McNally, in case he got away."

"I killed her!" Hart cried, clutching Nora to him.

"It was my fault," Kennedy proclaimed, shaking his head. "You tried to stop me, but I was too hasty. You knew it wasn't Trenary. You knew—" Suddenly he stopped, as if realizing what he was saying. "How did you know?" he asked, pulling Hart away from the body. "How?" he demanded.

Standing and looking up at Kennedy in despair, Hart clenched his fists and wailed in anguish, "Because *I* am Edward Trenary! *I'm* the one who paid McNally to wreck those trains!"

Kennedy suddenly dropped all pretense of ignorance. "We know that," he said coldly. "But we don't know why."

Hart cocked his head, looking at him queerly. "You know?"

"Ever since this afternoon, when our office printed Nora's pictures and identified you as the wealthy young Edward Trenary. They also found out that a supply of diethyl ether was shipped to you in Denver." He paused, allowing Hart time to understand the full weight of what he was saying, then continued, "We know who you are and what you did, but we don't know why. That's why Nora and I set up this . . . this little ruse."

His jaw dropping open, Hart spun back around and stared down at Nora. She had raised herself up on one elbow and was looking back at him.

"Nora!" he gasped.

"I'm sorry," she said as she sat up. "I tried to get you to confide in me—back at the hotel before you left. But you wouldn't."

"We needed proof," Kennedy went on, "so Nora searched your room after we left."

"That's where I found this wig and the powder you used to whiten your mustache. We're about the same size, so I borrowed one of your suits and made a mustache from a piece of the wig."

Hart just stood there shaking his head in disbelief. "But . . . but he shot you."

"No, I didn't," Kennedy interjected. "We planned in advance that if a buggy should appear with someone dressed like Trenary, I would fire into the air."

Nora stood now and took a cautious step toward Hart. "I had a small sack of red liquid that I poured onto the shirt as I was falling." She saw the pain in Hart's eyes and said, "I'm sorry. I didn't want it to end like this."

Hart's head lowered, and he began to nod. "You did what you had to do," he whispered. "I gave you no other choice."

"But why?" Nora asked, reaching out and tenderly touching his arm.

Hart shrugged. "I didn't need the money—I inherited plenty of it. But that seemed to be the only reason people cared about me, so I disappeared—changed my appearance—and became a reporter. I wanted people to respect me for my abilities."

"You engineered all of this just so that you could create a series of sensational news stories for yourself to cover?" Kennedy asked.

"It seemed like a good idea. I thought I had everything worked out so that no one would be hurt. And I was careful to cover my tracks."

"You mean the informer?" Nora asked.

"Yes." Hart chuckled. "I convinced one of McNally's men to sell me information so that I'd have a cover story in case someone guessed that I knew about the collisions ahead of time."

"It worked . . . for a time," Kennedy put in.

"Even if somebody figured out that Jim Hart and Edward Trenary were the same person, I never thought they'd connect us to McNally. After all, McNally didn't even know the name of the man who hired him. And that man was old—while Edward Trenary and Jim Hart are young."

"We'd better get back to the train," Kennedy said, taking Hart by the arm.

"I'm sorry," Hart apologized, looking back at Nora. "I never wanted anyone to get hurt."

"I believe you," Nora replied sincerely.

Kennedy started to lead him away, but Hart held back for a moment and called back to Nora, "If things had worked out differently. If I hadn't . . . Do you think there might have been a chance for us?"

Nora sighed and then slowly shook her head. "No, Jim. Perhaps at another time . . . in another place . . ."

Hart nodded, then smiled at her. "I understand," he whispered. Turning to Kennedy, he said, "I'm ready to go now," and started back to the train.

It was late morning by the time Stuart Kennedy and Nora Sutherland returned to the Orient Hotel in Denver. The operation had gone flawlessly, with Edward Trenary and the entire McNally gang in custody—including the members who were arrested aboard the westbound freight train by the Limon deputies. Best of all, the names of the Faraday agents had been kept out of all the news reports, and that would help in future undercover assignments.

Nora held Kennedy's arm as they entered the lobby. She no longer was wearing the business suit but had changed into her dress, which she had brought along in the buggy when she rode out to the crash site.

Glancing over at the dining room, Kennedy asked, "Would you like something to eat?"

"I just want to go to bed," she sighed. "It's been a long night."

"That it has," he agreed, leading her up the stairs.

"What do you think will become of him?" she asked as they made their way up to the third floor.

"Jim Hart?" Kennedy asked.

"Or Edward Trenary, I suppose—though it sounds strange."

"Undoubtedly he'll go to prison. They may charge him with murder, but I doubt that charge will stick. Probably he'll get out in ten years or so."

"He'll still be a young man—only in his thirties."

"Hopefully a wiser man, too," Kennedy added.

"He really took me by surprise," she admitted. "I never would have guessed . . ."

"It's harder to see the truth when you care about someone."

Nora stopped at the head of the stairs and looked up at him. "You didn't guess either," she said defensively.

"I know, Nora. I cared, too."

Nora smiled. "I'm sorry. I thought you were implying that my feelings might have been—"

"No," Kennedy said, squeezing her hand. "I trust you. I couldn't work with you if I didn't."

"Well, maybe someday a stranger *will* ride up and sweep me off my feet," she teased.

"I thought he already had."

"I don't know about that. . . ." she said coyly.

"You want to be swept off your feet?" he asked. Grinning, he reached behind her, lifted her in his arms, and carried her down the hall.

"My room or yours?" she asked, her tone alluring and suggestive.

"Mine. It's closer—and I left it unlocked." Reaching the door, he pushed it open and carried her over the threshold.

"Do I still have to pretend to be your widowed sister?" she asked, her hands caressing his hair.

"Didn't you notice?" Still carrying her, he raised his left hand to a position where she could see the gold band around his fourth finger. "I put it back on downstairs."

"Oh, Mr. Kennedy, I love you." She pulled his head close and kissed his neck.

"And I love you, *Mrs.* Kennedy." He turned and kicked the door shut, then carried his wife across the room to the big four-poster bed.

Watch for

THE GOLD TRAIN

next in the Faraday series
coming soon from
Lynx Books!